blue skies

blue skies

ANNE BUSTARD

Simon & Schuster Books for Young Readers

New York   London   Toronto   Sydney   New Delhi

SIMON & SCHUSTER BOOKS FOR YOUNG READERS
An imprint of Simon & Schuster Children's Publishing Division
1230 Avenue of the Americas, New York, New York 10020
This book is a work of fiction. Any references to historical events, real people, or real places are used fictitiously. Other names, characters, places, and events are products of the author's imagination, and any resemblance to actual events or places or persons, living or dead, is entirely coincidental.
Text © 2020 by Anne Bustard
Cover illustrations © 2020 by Dung Ho Hanh
Cover design by Lizzy Bromley © 2020 by Simon & Schuster, Inc.
All rights reserved, including the right of reproduction in whole or in part in any form.
SIMON & SCHUSTER BOOKS FOR YOUNG READERS
and related marks are trademarks of Simon & Schuster, Inc.
For information about special discounts for bulk purchases, please contact
Simon & Schuster Special Sales at 1-866-506-1949 or business@simonandschuster.com.
The Simon & Schuster Speakers Bureau can bring authors to your live event. For more information or to book an event, contact the Simon & Schuster Speakers Bureau at 1-866-248-3049 or visit our website at www.simonspeakers.com.
Also available in a Simon & Schuster Books for Young Readers hardcover edition
Interior design by Lizzy Bromley
The text for this book was set in Adobe Garamond Pro.
Manufactured in the United States of America 0221 OFF
First Simon & Schuster Books for Young Readers paperback edition March 2021
2 4 6 8 10 9 7 5 3 1
The Library of Congress has cataloged the hardcover edition as follows:
Names: Bustard, Anne, 1951– author.
Title: Blue skies / Anne Bustard.
Description: First edition. | New York : Simon & Schuster Books for Young Readers, [2020] |
Summary: France sends the Merci Train to the United States to thank America for helping France during and after WWII, and one of the train stops will be the small town of Gladiola, Texas, where ten-year-old Glory Bea hopes for the greatest miracle—that her missing-in-action father will be on the train. | Includes bibliographical references.
Identifiers: LCCN 2019006132 | ISBN 9781534446069 (hardcover : alk. paper)
ISBN 9781534446076 (pbk) | ISBN 9781534446083 (ebook)
Subjects: | CYAC: Loss (Psychology) | Fathers and daughters—Fiction. | Family life—Texas—Fiction.
| Texas—History—1846–1950—Fiction.
Classification: LCC PZ7.1.B89 Bl 2020 | DDC [Fic]—dc23
LC record available at https://lccn.loc.gov/2019006132

To Lane,

my miracle

one

MIRACLES HAPPEN in Gladiola, Texas, population 3,421.

And since Grams is responsible for thirty-nine so far, I'm counting on her gift to run in the family. After all, she always says, "Have audacious expectations."

Why not?

I want a miracle of my very own.

You see, my grams is the best matchmaker in the county. Her Wall of Fame proves it. Thirty-nine gold-framed photos of couples on their wedding days, including Mama and Daddy, fill our study wall. That averages out to one per year since she and Grandpa walked down the aisle. Some folks say it's a hobby. Grams says it's a calling.

Even though I'm only in fifth grade, and I don't know much about boys, and I've never made a match, I am positive that my best friend, Ruby Jane Pfluger, needs my help.

After all, she asked.

Call it destiny. Call it crazy. I answered the call.

Glory Bea Bennett, matchmaker extraordinaire, was born.

"Happily ever after," says Ruby Jane as we amble up the red carpet at the end of the Saturday picture show. She twists a lock of her cinnamon-colored hair around her finger. "That's how Ben Truman and I will live. Right?"

Once Daddy comes home, my family will too.

Ruby Jane's seen more movies than anyone else I know, and her favorites always end that way. Which is why today's feature didn't make her top ten. Ruby Jane's big dream makes sense. Can I guarantee it? I don't think Grams dares to make that whopper of a promise. "Wouldn't that be great?" I reply.

My answer must be good enough, because I swear I can see all of the braces in my best friend's mouth.

I can imagine Ruby Jane and Ben, my next-door neighbor, together, with their photograph displayed on my own Wall of Fame in my bedroom. Except her request is not without its challenges.

"Shy" doesn't begin to explain my naive friend.

Ben was king of his sixth-grade back-to-school dance this fall and Delilah Wallingham was the queen. Now Ruby Jane aims to take Delilah's place.

"Let me ask you something," I say as I catch a whiff of fruity bubble gum while we pass the next row of seats. "Have you talked to Ben? I mean, had a real conversation with him?"

"Of course. Every time . . . almost every time I see him."

"'Hi, Ben' is not a conversation, Ruby Jane."

"I know," she says, her forehead all wrinkly. "Now it's our first day of Christmas break, and I won't have a chance for more than two weeks."

"Don't worry. I believe in you and your sixth-grade heart-throb. I already have a plan. It starts right now. Today is Ben's first day at the soda fountain."

"I knew I could count on you, Glory Bea," says my closest friend, and she sprints ahead.

Miracle number forty, here we come.

And, I hope, a top-secret forty-first miracle too.

I stop halfway up the red carpet and clutch the charm bracelet Daddy handed me at the train station before he left.

I rub its shamrock for luck, close my eyes, and picture Daddy's big smile.

I refuse to believe what they say about him.

When you love someone, you never give up hope.

Not ever.

"Hurry up, Glory Bea," hollers Ruby Jane, and I open my eyes. My friend is only two steps away from the lobby. The smell of warm buttery popcorn fills the theater from the concession stand out front.

"On my way," I say.

But not before I pray for the umpteenth time for my family's happily ever after.

All the men in our town who went to the war came back.

Save one.

They say my daddy was lost in France on a beach called Omaha.

I am still waiting for him to be found.

two

MY DADDY'S SMILE is on my mind when Ruby Jane and I hop into McGrath's Pharmacy. This is one of Daddy's favorite places.

The counter at the soda fountain is jumping. Cherry, vanilla, and chocolate sugarcoat the air. High above the conversations, "Love Somebody" soars out of the jukebox. We take the last seats and I refocus.

"Welcome," says Ben as he zips by with an armload of dishes. "Good to see you, Ruby Jane. Glory Bea. I'll take your order ASAP."

"He's glad I'm here," whispers Ruby Jane. "He said my name."

I don't explain it's Ben's job to be extra friendly.

Ruby Jane stares at Ben as if she's never seen him before. Grams always says that's a sure sign someone is love-struck.

Which is why he doesn't look any different to me. Same short brown hair. Same dimpled chin. Same tallness. Though the white shirt, skinny black tie, and white hat are new.

Ben returns in a jiffy. "Let me guess," he says as he puts a paper napkin in front of each of us. "One Dr Pepper float?"

This is what it's like to live in a small town. People know you and your favorite foods, thanks to potlucks, picnics, and parties.

"You got it," I say. "Right, Ruby Jane?"

As Ben takes his receipt book out of his back pocket and his pencil from behind his ear, my first client clutches the counter with both hands. Finally, she nods. I understand the no-smile. Sometimes she's self-conscious about her braces.

Ben writes down our order and then leans toward us. "This just in," he says in a low voice while tapping his pencil on the counter like he is sending news over a teletype machine. "I predict the announcement I just heard about the Merci Train will be life changing." He salutes us. "Back on the double."

That's quite a forecast. Ben loves to imitate radio commentator Mr. Drew Pearson, who specializes in bold predictions. Plus, the man has connections to the Merci Train.

The Gratitude Train. The Thank You Train. It has lots of names. They all mean one thing: the people of France want to say thanks to the people of the United States for all our help, like my daddy's during the war. And for all our help afterward too.

Although the war ended more than three years ago, it'll take more money and more time for France to rebuild everything the Nazis destroyed. It doesn't help that their winters are extra cold. Some people haven't had enough food this whole time!

Last year, Mr. Pearson broadcast a solution called the Friendship Train. He asked Americans to fill up trainloads of food and ship them over to France and Italy. So we did.

Folks around here organized a canned milk drive. Grandpa was the captain of our block, and Ben and I were his assistants. All told, our town collected dozens of cases. The *Gladiola Gazette* took a picture of me standing on my tiptoes, trying to reach the top of the stacks loaded up on the train platform while Ben and Grandpa hoisted the first case.

Now, in return, a trainload of gifts from France is headed to the US, one boxcar for each state, plus one. Grandpa says he doesn't know what is being sent. They have to be special, because he calls them "gifts of love."

Just like that, Ben sets a float with two cherries on top between Ruby Jane and me. "The Texas boxcar is going to make a stop right here," he says, and hands us each a spoon.

"In Gladiola?" I say.

"Really?" asks Ruby Jane, and she takes a long sip of our float.

"Affirmative," says Ben.

Grandpa posted a map above our telephone that shows the route. Early next year the Texas boxcar will travel by ship from France to New Jersey, by rail to Fort Worth, and then down the tracks to Austin.

There must be an extra-special reason why it's not rushing right by us.

"Oh!" I say as a shiver starts at the top of my head and zings through me.

What if?

"You okay, Glory Bea?" my friends ask.

"Never better," I say, and wave my spoon.

It could happen.

I mean, why not this time?

I've always known that the day Daddy returns won't be ordinary. It would be on my birthday or Easter or the Fourth of July or his birthday or Mama's or Christmas. Or the day the Merci Train boxcar arrives from France!

Why else would it stop in Gladiola?

"Now, wait," I say, and point my spoon at Ben. "This better not be a joke. Today is December eighteenth, not April first."

"It's a fact, Glory Bea. Relayed by the top brass: the mayor and your grandpa."

A fact. I can live with *this* fact.

And that Ruby Jane spoke to Ben.

If I were in a movie musical, I'd jump on the counter and tap-dance right now. Only, I'm not in a musical. And I can't tap.

I know there's a chance I could be wrong about Daddy returning with the Merci boxcar. But Daddy will come home. I know I'm not mistaken about that.

"Plan as if something good is going to happen." That's Grandpa's motto. Coupled with "You can always change the plan."

So this time I'll pray even harder. I'll look for even more proof before I'm one hundred and ten percent sure. I won't tell Ruby Jane until I know. I can be patient. Besides, it's not like I've ever told anyone else. It's Daddy's and my secret secret.

I won't stop celebrating the possibility. I slip my spoon through the thick whipped topping, into the frosty vanilla ice cream floating in caramel-colored goodness, and up into my mouth. It is sweet mixed with sweet and sweeter—my definition of "divine." I go back to tap-dancing on the soda fountain counter.

three

"IT'S AN HONOR for us to be honored," Grandpa says at the dinner table as he takes a serving of the pale green beans Mama fixed. "It's not every day something comes to us all the way from France."

Or somebody.

I look at the empty chair between Grams and me. The chair no one sits in, even when we have company. Daddy's chair.

"What can I do to help, sir?" asks Ben. He's still in his soda fountain uniform, minus the hat.

I catch Mama's eye, and she winks. Ben and Grandpa have been good buddies since forever. "Like white on rice," says Grams. You might think that would've changed when Ben's dad came back from the war. What changed instead was Ben's dad, so Ben and Grandpa are still close. "Can I count on your assistance with the parade?" asks Grandpa.

"Ready and able, sir," says Ben, and shovels a forkful of meat loaf into his mouth.

He chews, takes in some tea, chews a bunch more, and finally swallows.

All that chomping tells me everything I need to know. It doesn't smell burnt, but I reach for the ketchup and smother my meat loaf with it anyway. I top the crusty brown mac and cheese with some too, just in case. Thank goodness Grams only lets Mama cook dinner once a week. Otherwise, we might starve.

Ben has already eaten at our house twice this week. Grams started inviting him over last month after his daddy lost another security guard job and went to the hospital. Every year, the weeks leading up to December 7 and beyond are sorrowful for Mr. Truman. Come early January, he always improves. This go-round he stopped talking. Now Ben's mama works extra shifts, and Ben's been eating here.

I'd wager Ben's job money isn't for his own spending, even though ever since his brother enlisted, he sends part of his paycheck home.

I lean over and take a sip from my straw. Air. I pucker up and try again. The straw squeaks and squeals. Suddenly, sticky sweet tea spurts from side holes near the top.

"Would you look at that," says Grams.

"Ben Truman!" I holler, dabbing up the tea with my napkin. I pull the straw out of the glass and fling it across the table at him. "You are in so much trouble."

Grandpa leans over with a smile. "Return fire," he says real low.

I push back my chair. "Anyone need anything while I'm up?" I ask as casually as possible.

Everyone bows their heads, although I know they aren't praying. They're trying to hide their smiles.

I crumple my napkin over my glass with one hand, grab an ice cube with the other, and stroll around the table.

"Touché," I say, and slip the cube down Ben's collar.

"Truce!" he shouts, and shakes the back of his shirt. The ice falls to the floor and slides away.

"Promise?" I ask.

"Scout's honor," he says, and holds up two fingers.

I put my hands on my waist. "Since when did you become a Scout?"

Ben shrugs. "Since now."

I get another straw and sit back down. My plate of food is downright pitiful. At least there is dessert. Grams has made her famous pecan pie.

Everyone talks about the likelihood of snow for the holidays. It has never, not once, snowed in Gladiola, Texas, on Christmas Day.

"Miracles happen," says Grams.

That I believe.

Last month an article in the *Gladiola Gazette* reported that a man from Tula, Texas, showed up after disappearing twelve years ago. He'd been hurt in an out-of-town accident in Chicago and got amnesia. When his memory came back, he found his way home. Grams called it "a feel-good story if there ever was one."

My daddy's story will be even better.

Maybe he got amnesia too and has been living in France for the past four and a half years as someone else. And is finding his way back right now.

"When did you say the Merci boxcar is coming?" I ask.

"We don't know the exact date," says Grandpa. "Its ETA is the middle of February."

"Valentine's Day?" My hands reach for my heart.

"Possibly."

"Oh, Grandpa, that would be perfect."

As in, I couldn't have planned it any better myself.

"Well, now that we've got that settled," says Grams, placing her napkin on the table. "Let's move to the parlor for dessert, before William and I go to the Christmas party in . . ."

Grandpa takes his gold watch out of his pocket. "Twenty-three minutes." Grandpa likes to be precise. He is a retired railroad man and thinks it's best when everything runs on schedule.

Ding dong.

"I'll get it," I say. We aren't expecting more company. Only, if I have to guess, it's the McGraths, Grams and Grandpa's best friends and our across-the-street neighbors. The couples are double-dating to the party.

"Merry Christmas, almost," I sing as I swing open the door.

Colder-than-cold air rushes in. At dinner Grandpa said it'd dropped thirty degrees since this afternoon.

"Oh." I stumble back a step and grab the doorknob with both hands so I won't fall.

I squint into the bright light on the porch. A tall man with short dark hair stands before me. He holds his hat in one hand and a bouquet of flowers in the other—lilies: Mama's favorite.

My heart thumps hard. I blink until my eyes adjust and stare into his face.

"Glory Bea?" he asks.

I squeeze my eyes closed and press my lips together, the cold air spreading goose bumps across my arms and down my legs.

The accent tells me that this man is from up north.

"Who is it?" asks Mama, appearing beside me.

"Randall Horton," says the man, holding out the sweet-smelling flowers.

Mama's hands fly to her mouth and her eyes soften. She puts an arm around me and hugs me close. It's not enough to warm me up.

"Glory Bea," she says, her voice quivering, "I'd like you to meet your daddy's best friend in the service."

"It's taken me too long," says Randall Horton in a rush. "George and I made a promise to visit one another's families if . . ." Randall Horton takes a gulp of air. "Well," he says, looking into Mama's eyes, "I finally made it."

Grandpa lets out a big sigh behind me. I wiggle away from Mama and back up. I'm freezing. Grams and Mama hug Randall Horton on either side and sway back and forth. He puts his arms around their shoulders and squeezes tight.

"Welcome," says Grams. "Welcome home."

four

I KNOW WHO Randall Horton is. Mama keeps his letters in a big wooden box right next to Daddy's. There are five from Randall Horton. He's written her each Thanksgiving since my daddy landed on that beach. Mama read every one to me.

Sometimes at night when I can't sleep, I tiptoe downstairs for milk and one of Grams's cookies, and Mama will be sitting in Daddy's leather chair in the parlor, reading a letter from him or one of Randall Horton's November letters. The first came from France; last month's from New York.

At school we learned how to write a business letter, a formal letter, an informal letter, a letter to the editor, and a thank-you letter. The words are different each time; Randall Horton always writes the same kind. He says how grateful he is to have known my daddy. He says that every day, not just

Thanksgiving, he is thankful for his friendship. At the end of each letter he asks Mama to send his greetings to Grams, Grandpa, and me.

Now everyone takes a seat in the parlor, where Grandpa's paintings of bluebonnets hang on every wall. Except me. Two of the paintings are crooked, and I even them up.

Mama and Grams sit on the sofa. Randall Horton and Grandpa sit on the blue wing chairs on either side. I claim the leather chair across the room.

"All the way from Brooklyn, New York," says Mama to Randall Horton. "You must be exhausted."

"Nothing like a warm welcome to solve that," he says.

I roll my eyes.

"Glory Bea," says Grams as she reaches for one of the cups on the coffee table, "will you bring us what we need for dessert?"

Any excuse to leave is fine by me—though I don't want to miss a word, so I dash to the kitchen. The dirty dishes are scraped and stacked by the sink. A note on the top plate reads—*Thanks for dinner. –Ben.*

I forgot all about him.

I collect the dessert plates and forks on the kitchen table and scurry back.

"So you've got kin spread from coast to coast," says Grandpa to Randall Horton as I set the plates down.

"Yes, sir."

"How wonderful you can see your sister in Florida for the holidays," says Grams while she cuts her pie.

"Yes, indeed. I'm just passing through."

That's the first good news I've heard since he walked in.

I shuttle dessert and coffee for Grams and finally sit back down.

"Mrs. Bennett, this is the best pecan pie I've ever had."

Grams beams. It's her blue-ribbon special, made with pecans from our very own trees.

"Hear, hear," says Grandpa, and raises his coffee cup in a toast.

"We pronounce it 'pea-*con*,'" I say, and shove a forkful of the gooey, nutty goodness into my mouth. "Pea-*can*" sounds like fingernails on a chalkboard.

"I appreciate the intel," says Randall Horton.

Mama raises her eyebrows.

I fake smile back.

After a few more bites, Grandpa sets his fork on his empty plate. "We're on our way to a holiday open house, and we'd be pleased to have you join us, Randall. Folks will be happy to make your acquaintance, and we can continue this conversation down the street."

Say yes, Randall Horton; it's time for Mama and me to roll our hair and play Hearts. I can always count on Grandpa to come up with a good idea.

"You'll be our special guest," says Grams.

"I'd like that," he says.

"Lila June," says Grams, "we'll wait for you to change."

Mama never goes to parties. She says, *No, thank you*, no matter who it is or how many times she's asked. Mama never gives a reason and I know what it is. She's waiting on Daddy.

Mama wiggles her fingers on top of her knees. "Oh, I don't know."

I twist my mouth.

Her fingers still and she gives her knees a quick pat. "Maybe I will."

"But . . . ," I start. Only, no one hears me.

Mama pops up and gives me a kiss on the top of my head. "I won't be long," she says, and hurries away.

I stomp to the kitchen, turn on the hot water at the sink full blast, and stuff in the plunger. I pour in gobs of detergent and stir up suds until my hands hurt from the heat.

Mama isn't being Mama. What is she thinking?

I scrub away the question I don't have an answer for and think about my daddy.

He's easy to remember. We talk about him a bunch, and all of his belongings are still in the house. Like his overcoat in the downstairs closet, chessboard in the study, clothes in the bedroom, shaving brush in the medicine chest, and pocket change on the bureau. It's all right here, keeping us company and waiting for his return.

The swinging door to the kitchen opens. "We're off," says

Mama. She's wearing a poofy emerald-green dress, and she's put her hair in an updo. I catch a whiff of perfume. Usually she smells like Ivory soap. "I'll ask Ben to come back over so you won't be alone."

"Don't bother," I holler as the door swings closed.

five

I DON'T DALLY with the dishes. In minutes I have on my winter coat and am out the front door, headed toward town. Right into the wind. I turn up my collar and march ahead. Big red bows, gold ornaments, and candy canes decorate Christmas wreaths on the doors of almost every house on either side of our street.

The mayor's house on the corner of Azalea and Main is all lit up, both inside and out. The drapes over the windows are open, and grown-ups stand around in clumps in the living room.

I can't see Mama.

In my rush, I forgot my gloves. I stuff my hands deeper into my pockets, hoping to claim warmth, and creep around to the side yard. Prickly holly bushes snag at my coat; I pay them no mind as I peek in a window.

Mama and Randall Horton stand side by side near the piano. Talking. Smiling.

My stomach flip-flops.

"Good e-ven-ing," says a deep voice behind me.

I scream. Kind of sort of loud.

I whip around while my heart ticks extra beats.

Two twisted mouths and noses, all lit up, float before me. One is Ben's. The other is his friend Harry Ackerman's.

"Y'all scared me," I say.

I suck in a big old lungful of air just as the window behind me flies open. "Everything okay out there?"

Click. Thud. The faces vanish. Running footsteps and muted laughter heads into the darkness. I turn to see the mayor and Mr. McGrath leaning out of the window.

"It's just me, Glory Bea," I say, slowing my heart. "Wilson got out and I chased him into this yard and I . . . I tripped."

It could have been true. Last year Ben's dog snuck in through the kitchen door before this very party, nabbed the ham, and hightailed it back home with his feast. His escapade was written up in the newspaper and made him famous and infamous.

"Be careful now," says Mr. Crowley. "It's chilly out there. And don't forget your flashlight."

"Thanks," I say, and look around. A tiny spot of light shines on the edge of the lawn and I stomp over to pick it up.

One of these days, Ben Truman. One of these days . . .

Before I land in the leather chair in the parlor, I toss the flashlight onto Ben's front doormat as I fly home. Then I pull the soft holiday throw Grams quilted around my body to warm up. Peppermint candy canes and pine scent the room.

Daddy made the wooden star on top of our Christmas tree when he was in seventh-grade shop. The yellow paint isn't as bright as it used to be and some of it has flaked off. As Grams says, it has character.

When I was two, Mama, Daddy, and me moved in with Grams and Grandpa. Ever since, after the strings of lights were wrapped around and around, and all of our ornaments were in place, Daddy and I would waltz and jitterbug and cha-cha-cha to Christmas carols. I remember, because Grandpa has kept up the tradition.

Then we'd eat Grams's fresh-from-the-oven gingerbread cookies.

Ding dong.

Mama wouldn't ring the bell before walking in.

I waltz to the door. It's Ben. "I don't need you," I say, and slam the door.

I plop back into the leather chair in the parlor and resettle under the quilt.

I close my eyes and play the decorating-the-tree-with-Daddy movie over and over.

I must have fallen asleep because the next thing I know the front door is opening. The clock on the mantel says ten. They've been gone more than three whole hours.

"What a day!" says Grams. "A day of many blessings."

She starts to hum "Silent Night."

I jump up and peek around the wall. Good. No Randall Horton.

"I expect she'll be right in," Grams says, reading the question about Mama in my eyes.

"Where is *he* staying?" I ask aloud.

"The McGraths insisted Randall sleep in their spare bedroom rather than at the motel by the highway," Grams says.

I make an ugly face.

"He's a fine man," counters Grandpa.

I rub my arms to take off the chill that just entered.

"It's easy to see why Randall and our George were such good friends," Grandpa continues, and holds up his elbow. Grams slips her arm into his and gives it a pat. "I especially miss him this time of year," she says.

"Me too," says Grandpa.

I reach my arms around my grandparents. They smell like gingerbread, all vanilla and spice, and I hug even tighter.

"Looky here," says Grams, gently tugging at the end of my ponytail. "A leaf."

"Sure enough," says Grandpa.

"I had to go out for just a minute," I say.

"So we heard," says Grams, and starts humming again.

"Off to bed, sugar," Mama says as she walks in. "It's late, even for holiday bedtimes. I thanked Ben for coming over, though it looks to me like he was bundled up good on the porch the whole time."

Ben stayed? "That was his choice," I say.

I scoot up to my room. Daddy's photo stands front and center on the top of my dresser. He's wearing his US Army Ranger uniform and a big smile. I like his twinkly eyes the best.

Three shiny buttons march down the front of his jacket, and his cap fits snug over his short dark hair. He stands tall beside the pecan tree in our front yard on a blue-sky day, his smile just for me.

Daddy and me spent that entire afternoon walking around Gladiola. I snapped pictures of him at all our favorite spots. I used up the whole roll of film, all twelve shots. This was the one that turned out best.

"See you soon," I say, I hope, I pray. "Real soon." And I blow him a good night kiss.

Then I move to my front window and look up. The sky is cloudy and I can't see any stars.

Across the street, the McGraths' living room curtains are open, and Randall Horton sits in an easy chair next to the fireplace.

I yank my curtains closed and go to bed.

six

ONE LONG RING, a short ring, and another long one. That's
our phone line. We all know it's for Grams. It is love call time.
Even on a Sunday morning. The days leading up to New Year's
and Valentine's are high season.

"Tell them I'll be right there, Glory Bea," says Grams as she
pours herself a cup of coffee.

I run to the hallway and lift the receiver from the wall phone.

A *National Geographic* map of the world is thumbtacked next
to the phone. A red pencil line runs across the Atlantic Ocean
from France to New Jersey, with three other lines that move up
and down and across our country. Fort Worth, Gladiola, and
Austin are starred. I'd bet money that in the coming days, the
map will be dotted with pushpins, noting the location of the
Merci Train travels.

"Bennett residence," I say.

"*Bonjour*, Glory Bea," says Miss Connie, our telephone operator. Ever since the news of the boxcar, she's been flavoring her language with French.

Grandpa has already tapped her as his transportation coordinator for the parade. She'll make sure there are enough fancy cars for the mayor, town council, and special guests to ride in. And if they don't want a car, she'll round them up a nice horse.

"This call's for you, *chérie*," says Miss Connie.

There's a brief pause. "Did Ben say anything about me at dinner last night?" asks Ruby Jane.

"No, but that doesn't mean a thing." At least I think it doesn't. Ben didn't mention Delilah, either.

We replay each and every word of yesterday's soda fountain visit before Miss Connie interrupts us. "There's a call for your grandmother."

"One moment, please," I say, trying to sound official, and tell Ruby Jane good-bye.

I return with Grams, hand her the receiver, and walk away as slow as possible.

Maybe I'll learn some matchmaking tips.

"How old is he?" says Grams as she opens up her journal.

Grams only matches old people. If they haven't found someone on their own by the time they are thirty, or are starting over, she is happy to provide a little extra help.

"Any children?" she asks, and writes something down. "Has a pig as a pet. That's one I haven't heard before. What else?"

People call Grams when someone single moves to these parts or is widowed. She reads the obituaries every week. She's even had offers to go commercial, though Grams always says no thanks. She considers her calling a community service.

The best match she ever made? Mama and Daddy.

As the story goes, Grams and Grandpa were at the How-Dee-Do Drive-In one Saturday afternoon in Gerbera, a few towns over, when Mama skated up and took their order. It was her junior year in high school and she'd just moved to town. Grams thought she was cuter than a speckled pup and flat out asked if she had a beau. Next thing you know, my daddy went calling. They said it was love at first sight.

To my knowledge it was the only time Grams made an exception to her old-people rule.

Grams returns to the kitchen, and the phone rings again. I remove her half-eaten breakfast and fork and follow her to the hallway. She'll need her strength for back-to-back calls.

Between long pauses and bites of egg she says, "Oh. Uh-huh," and "I see."

I'm barely back in the kitchen when Grams brings her empty plate to the sideboard. Her eyes are extra big. "I'm off to a quick visit before church," she says. "Someone is on her third piece of chocolate cake. For breakfast."

"Sounds like a love emergency," Grandpa says as Grams leaves the room. He rubs his hands together and reaches for the plate of bacon.

Mama raises her eyebrows and I smile.

"It was good to see you out last night, Lila June," says Grandpa.

Quick as a hiccup, my milk curdles in my stomach.

I excuse myself and go upstairs to get ready for church. But first I sit at my desk. Miss Connie has given me an idea. With Grandpa's motto in mind, I plan as if something good will happen.

I locate a fresh sheet of paper, pick up my pen, and in my best cursive, write a letter to the editor of the *Gladiola Gazette*.

December 19, 1948

Dear Mr. Wyatt,
You run a very fine weekly newspaper. I have a proposal for making it even better—feature French words or phrases in each edition until the Texas Merci boxcar arrives.
Let's celebrate with flair.

Your faithful reader,
Glory Bea Bennett
P.S. I would like to suggest that the first word be "welcome."

What I didn't write was how welcoming it will be for Daddy to hear folks speak French.

seven

NOT EVERYTHING can be planned, especially where love is concerned. That's why Grams says, "Be open to the possibilities."

Let's hope Ruby Jane agrees.

"Come now," I tell her, on the phone later that afternoon. "Take the shortcut."

That's our code.

Grandpa timed us once. If we take the streets, we can make it door to door in two and a half minutes. Cutting through yards shaves fifty-nine seconds.

In ninety-one seconds I open the back door. It's still nippy, yet the sun streams in. "Ben's in his front yard," I say.

Ruby Jane squeals.

"Smile, wave, and say three words. Think of yourself as an actress."

"All right," Ruby Jane says, and pinches her cheeks for

color like she saw Judy Garland do on the silver screen, as we head through my house to the front yard.

As we close the front door, Ben attacks the leaves beside our shared picket fence with his rake. He looks a little out of sorts. He's wearing his older brother's high school letter sweater.

Ben, Gary, and their dad always made clearing leaves a game. Gary is still stationed overseas so Ben is on his own now.

He leans on his rake and surveys the leaves piled in a line as straight as the soda fountain counter.

Ruby Jane and I tiptoe down the steps.

The wind kicks up, scattering some of Ben's work. His shoulders slump.

Wham! slams a door, and Randall Horton rushes across the street, waves at Ben, and dashes up the walkway. Before he can knock, Mr. Truman flings the door open.

Ben's dad is back? He must have returned today.

Mr. Truman wears his sailor uniform. He steps outside and yells, "ALL HANDS ON DECK." Randall Horton takes Mr. Truman's arm and ushers him back into his house.

Ruby Jane and I turn to each other and wince.

Ben stiffens and shakes his head.

Maybe Ruby Jane and I will be a welcome distraction. We stop when we reach the edge of his yard. I wrap my wool scarf around my neck and stand behind my friend. I remind her to breathe. When Ben finally turns, I wave, as Texas friendly as I can. He salutes us back.

"HOW ARE YOU?" Ruby Jane hollers louder than loud. Nerves can do that.

Wilson bounds up to Ben with a tennis ball, scattering even more leaves. Ben throws the ball, waves at us, and follows his collie.

"He noticed me. Again," says Ruby Jane as she whirls around. One of her pigtails catches on her braces as she smiles, and she brushes it away.

"He most certainly did." Ruby Jane will live on this for a week. "Good job."

Matchmaking is easy once you know what to do. I wish helping Ben's dad was too.

After a quick detour to the newspaper office to drop my letter through their mail slot, Ruby Jane and I arrive at her house in time for supper. Her younger brother, Homer, is already in his railroad pajamas. A matching blue-and-white striped cap tops his head.

Ruby Jane's mama felt guilty because Ruby Jane had to babysit Homer most of the afternoon, and no matter what she did, she couldn't make him stop telling the same joke: "What does a train say when it has a cold?" he asked. "Ah-choo-choo-choo-choo-choo."

So Mrs. Pfluger made Ruby Jane's favorite dessert, apple brown Betty. It smells delicious and looks like it could have come out of a page in the *Ladies' Home Journal*. Like Grams,

Mrs. Pfluger makes cooking look easy. She says the recipe is foolproof. Maybe she could share it with Mama.

Homer tells me his joke only three times. I would have listened to it three thousand, because all Mr. and Mrs. Pfluger talk about is Randall Horton.

"He fit right in, didn't he?" asks Mrs. Pfluger. Only it isn't a question. "Why, when he sat down at that piano and played, it seemed like we'd been singing Christmas carols with him forever. Did you hear his voice? He'd make a five-star addition to the Gladiola Glee Club."

"I've got to give the man a lot of credit, Penny," says Mr. Pfluger. "Re-upping for another tour of duty after all he'd seen. That took courage."

"Imagine," says Mrs. Pfluger. "Coming all this way to see Lila June."

Thank goodness Randall Horton is leaving tomorrow.

Did You Know?
Gladiola Gazette
December 22, 1948

Are we lucky ducks, or what?

I have it on good authority that
our town was designated the one and
only official stop of the Texas Merci
boxcar between its drop-off in Fort
Worth and final destination in Austin.
Our spectacular and long-standing state
reputation for hosting the "Best Small-Town
Fourth of July Parade" makes this possible.

Thank you, Mayor John Crowley, and
your wife, the ever-lovely Mrs. Geraldine
Crowley, for all of your efforts on our
behalf.

First, this potpourri of facts about the
Merci Train. It totals 49 forty-and-eight
boxcars, built to hold 40 men or 8 horses.
They were used in both world wars. Each
state will receive one, and the Territory
of Hawaii and the District of Columbia
will share one. The boxcars have been
refurbished and are filled to the brim with
gifts such as children's toys, needlework,

and books. Each one contains a wedding dress from seamstresses in Leon, and from French president Vincent Auriol, a rare Sèvres vase.

I for one can't wait to travel to Austin to see the gifts firsthand.

Second, plans are under way to welcome our state's boxcar in fine fashion. Please lend a hand. Committees have already been formed, and help is needed in all areas. Contact the following persons by phone to volunteer:

Transportation: Miss Connie Partridge, just pick up the phone and she'll answer

Main Street Decorations: Mr. Mark Ambrose, #68

Parade Floats & Bands, Etc.: Mr. William Bennett, #35

Potluck Bar-B-Que: Mrs. Helen Andrews, #18

Call now.

So now you know, dear Gladies, now you know,

Penny Pfluger

PS: Glory Bea, "*bienvenue*" means "welcome" in French.

eight

THE FIRST CHRISTMAS after Daddy left was the worst. Grandpa did not dress up as Santa at the hospital. Grams did not gift her famous pecan pies. Mama did not craft star ornaments out of wax. The Christmas tree in the parlor turned brown and dropped needles way before the twenty-fifth because I forgot to water it.

This Christmas might be the second worst.

Randall Horton did not get on that bus to Florida.

Instead, he is squished next to Grandpa, Mama, and me in the fifth row of Main Street Baptist, the biggest church in town, for the Gladiola Glee Club holiday concert.

I *should* be grateful. Randall Horton won't be at our Christmas dinner the day after tomorrow. He accepted an offer from the Crowleys instead.

Mama squashes me from the left, into the hard pew arm

on my right. Any more pressure and I might burst.

She points to "Douce Nuit" in the program. "This must be why your grandmother has been humming 'Silent Night.' Same tune, different words."

"I don't know it," I say. "It's . . ."

"French," says Mama. "I took a year of it in high school."

I twist around. "Do you still remember how to speak it?"

"I bet if I had someone to practice with," she says, and taps me on the nose, "I'd do just fine."

I'd tell her who, only I don't want to ruin Daddy's surprise. Plus, I need a little more proof that he's really coming this time.

Folks form a line to shake Randall Horton's hand. More than one says, "For a second, I thought you could have been George."

My daddy is taller. I'm sure Daddy can run faster, seeing as he was a track star, and sing better too. He would wake me up every morning with a song.

"It's too crowded," I say to Mama.

"Take off your coat, sweetie."

"I want to sit somewhere else."

Mama entwines her arm in mine as the organ prelude begins. "Please, stay." She's wearing perfume again. It smells like the gardenia corsage Grandpa gave Grams on their anniversary this year.

I wriggle, and Mama tightens her grip. "The First Noel" fills me with warmth and I give in.

Halfway through the concert, Grams walks to the podium. As the piano plays a lively intro, Grams puts on pipe cleaner antlers and begins to sing about Rudolph.

Someone in the first row starts swaying, and pretty soon the whole church is rocking side to side. We join in on the last line, ". . . You'll go down in his-toe-reee."

Grams bows as we whistle and clap. She points right at Grandpa and winks.

Grandpa touches his hand to his heart and returns the gesture, pointing right back at her. Randall Horton leans over and says something in Mama's ear. She nods and her shoulders shake just a little.

Daddy always says it is rude to tell secrets in public because it makes people feel left out.

Randall Horton laughs too loud and too long.

"Thank you for your enthusiasm," says Mr. McGrath, aka the glee club director, as we settle down. He tips his head back and closes his eyes before he continues. "Since 1943, when this next song was recorded by Bing Crosby, the Gladiola Glee Club, in honor of those who served in the war, has sung it at this concert. We send our thoughts to the families of those loved ones who will never return to us." He pauses and looks right at me. Some people do not have enough faith. "And now, 'I'll Be Home for Christmas.'"

Folks from the row behind us lay their hands on Mama's and my shoulders. Mama kisses the top of my head and sighs. Not a heavy sigh, more like a wish-upon-a-star sigh.

She is thinking about Daddy too, isn't she?

nine

I GRIP THE SMALL ball-shaped finial at the top of our banister with both hands, swing my left leg over the railing, lean forward, and let go. For a second. With my arms extended over my head, I cup my hands around the smooth, slick wood and inch my way downstairs. It isn't pretty, but I make it.

Grams chats nearby on the hall phone.

"More than a week?" she says to the caller. "Not to worry. Everyone's on a different schedule over the holidays and it's only two days after Christmas." Grams takes a sip of coffee and continues, "Sometimes absence makes the heart grow fonder."

My thoughts exactly. I am counting on this for Ben and Ruby Jane. Every Pfluger except Mr. Pfluger is still out of town visiting relatives.

I surmise that before Ruby Jane sees Ben again, she needs to know more about him in order to spark engaging conversation. It's time for his official interview.

First, I poke my head into the study, where I'd last seen Mama. She stands before the Wall of Fame. Her hand touches the photograph in the center: the one of her and Daddy. Seated in the back seat of a car in their wedding finery, she and Daddy pose for the photographer. They look so happy.

Mama's lips start to move, and I inch closer.

"You've been gone such a long, long time, George. I will always miss you."

No, Mama. You will not miss him forever. He is coming back. In less than two months.

Believe, Mama. Believe.

There's a reason Grams needlepointed the pillow on the wing chair after Daddy left that reads: NEVER GIVE UP. NEVER EVER, EVER GIVE UP.

I tiptoe back, take a few loud steps into the room, and tell Mama my plans.

"Don't spoil your dinner, honey. Your grandmother's cooking. And if you'd like, we could talk in French when you come back. *Oui?*"

"*Oui,*" I say, and kiss her on both cheeks like I hear they do in France.

I take the last empty red stool next to the window at the soda fountain, set my spiral notebook on the counter, and nod to

Delilah Wallingham beside me. She wiggles her fingers hi. As she inches her silver baton closer to her strawberry malt, she tells the stranger on her left, "I was queen, and Ben here was king."

Delilah was also voted most beautiful and most likely to succeed in Hollywood, though she's never been onstage. Maybe twirling in a parade counts.

"The usual, Glory Bea?" asks Ben.

"Just a regular DP, please," I say. "By the way, do you like girls with straight hair or curly hair the best?"

"Curly."

Delilah fluffs her wavy blond hair. I write down *curly*.

"Where do you like to sit when you watch a movie?"

"Right in the middle."

"Your favorite radio show besides *Drew Pearson Comments*?"

"What's up with the twenty questions?"

"Homework," I say. "I'm guessing *Abbott and Costello*?"

I've heard Ben toss lines with Grandpa from the comedians' baseball routine about who's on first.

"Negative," says Ben. *"Captain Midnight."* He points his thumb toward the other end of the counter and hurries away.

That was my daddy's favorite. Sometimes I wonder if the reason he hasn't come back yet is because he's a secret agent for real, not like on the radio. And until his job is done, he isn't allowed any contact with us. Until February.

Frank Sinatra croons on the jukebox about never smiling

again. Delilah stirs her malt. "Homework over the holidays?"

"Extra credit," I say.

Delilah readjusts the baby-blue sweater on her shoulders. The rhinestone sweater guard catches a ray of sunlight, and sparkles bounce across the ceiling.

I hunker over my spiral and doodle train boxcars, while Delilah describes her twirling lessons to the visitor, complete with an unauthorized demonstration. Ever since Delilah knocked over bottles of Pepto-Bismol, Mr. McGrath posted a sign in the window: NO BATON TWIRLING ALLOWED. I guess Delilah doesn't think it means her.

"I predict you'll like this, Glory Bea," says Ben as he serves me my soda. He leaves before I can ask another question.

"Word is," says Delilah, leaning closer as I take a long sip of my extra cold drink, "there's a certain Mr. Randall Horton that's been visiting your house. As in every day that ends with *y*. Keeping late hours too. Why, when he took your mama all the way to Austin for dinner, I heard they didn't get back until after midnight."

As if it were any of her business, Mama and Randall Horton had a meal with Mama's college roommate. Austin's under an hour's drive away and they were gone only a total of five. Delilah makes it sounds like they were on a date or something.

I swallow my mouthful of DP all at once. Icy jabs shoot up my head and stab each temple.

"My aunt in San Antonio remarried a year after her husband died in the war," says Delilah, and she taps a finger on her baton. "I was a junior bridesmaid and we stayed in a motel with a swimming pool. I guess your mama is a little slow."

I turn and glare. "You do not know everything there is to know, Delilah Wallingham."

Sure, we had a service for Daddy. Except he wasn't there.

Delilah laughs. "Whatever you say, Glory Bea Bennett."

There's a reason they call it "MIA, Missing in Action." It means Daddy can be found. Only, now I think he's going to find us.

"I've got to go." I count out the money for my soda plus tip in my shaky hands and place it on the counter.

"What about your extra credit?" asks Delilah. "And your soda?"

I try to smile.

Delilah is a know-it-all. So Ruby Jane and I don't hang out with her all the time. But I do need to be friendly on account of Mama. Delilah's daddy is her boss.

But she is not mine.

I do not want to talk about Randall Horton. That man has overstayed his welcome. Grams always says fish and company stink after three days. It is time for Randall Horton to see his sister in Florida and make his way back to New York.

We have to get ready for Daddy, and Randall Horton is starting to stink.

I trudge home, keeping my eyes on the sidewalk so I won't step on any cracks. I clutch my spiral across my chest. Someone has to do something.

Randall Horton isn't my only worry. I need more answers from Ben. Ruby Jane will expect a progress report upon her return. I'm not about to let her down.

At the corner of Azalea and Main, it comes to me.

I take off, and within seconds, I pound on Ben's front door. There's no car in the driveway. If his mama or dad is home, I can finish my questions.

Ben's dad answers, scowling.

"Sorry I knocked so hard."

Mr. Truman wears a long brown plaid bathrobe over his pajamas, and a heavy heart. I don't think he shaved this morning.

"Ben's not here," he says, and shuts the door.

I will not give up. No, not me.

The air cools, and I button up my coat.

According to Grams, before the war, Mr. Truman coached the high school baseball team in his free time and made the best Bar-B-Que sauce and brisket in Gladiola. He served as a cook on a battleship stationed in Pearl Harbor. Then the bombs fell. Ships sank. Sailors died.

Loud noises startle him.

I wish I hadn't banged the door.

Important French Words and Phrases (According to Mama)

1. *Bienvenue* (Be en va nu) Welcome
2. *Merci beaucoup* (Mare see boe coo) Thank you very much
3. *Comment allez-vous?* (Comahn tally vu) How are you?
4. *Très bien, merci!* (Tray be en, mare see) Very good, thank you!
5. *S'il vous plaît* (See voo play) Please
6. *Moi* (Mwa) Me
7. *Au revoir* (O rev wah) Good-bye
8. *Bon voyage* (Bohn voy ahj) Good-bye
9. *Fantastique* (Fawn tas teek) Fantastic
10. *C'est bon* (Say bohn) It's good

Did You Know?
Gladiola Gazette
December 29, 1948

Gladies, I am not the only one thinking
ahead, *oui*?

As this is my final column for the year,
let me be the first to wish you Happy New
Year, *Bonne année*!

In honor of a New Year's Eve tradition
in France, I will plant myself under
mistletoe for a kiss. Needless to say, my
family and I will still partake of black-
eyed peas on the first. Why not receive
double luck?

With a nod to the journalist Mr. Drew
Pearson, I submit this sampling of our
fair citizens' and esteemed visitors'
predictions for 1949:

Mrs. Geraldine Crowley: The Merci boxcar
will bring an unexpected blessing.

Mr. Steven McGrath: I will retire.

Mr. Randall Horton: The Brooklyn Dodgers
will win the World Series.

Mrs. George Bennett: Someone we all know
and love will marry.

Ben Truman: My brother will come home on leave.

Delilah Wallingham: I'll lead the Fourth of July parade.

Moi: A Gladiola citizen will audition for *Arthur Godfrey's Talent Scouts*.

So now you know, dear Gladies, now you know,

Penny Pfluger

PS: COMING SOON: Watch for an occasional French lesson or two via this column starting next week.

ten

RANDALL HORTON is at our house. Again.

Mama freshened the arrangement on the piano with new sprigs of fir. The silver and gold ball ornaments nestled among them catch the light of the candles on either side.

"It is a pleasure to be here, Mrs. Bennett," says Randall Horton as Grandpa shuffles and deals the deck of cards.

In the background, "Comin' in on a Wing and a Prayer" plays on the radio.

My prayer is that Randall Horton says good-bye to our town tonight. It's December 29 and he's still here.

Grams says prayers are answered in three ways—yes, no, and not now. This one needs to be yes.

"Everyone has made me feel so welcome here," Randall Horton says as he picks up his cards. "Especially all of you."

"Everybody wants to hear your story," says Mama.

"Main Street Baptist last night," says Grams, "the fish fry at the fire station tomorrow . . ."

". . . invites to lunches and dinners all week," adds Grandpa.

I throw down a card. He's staying that long?

"It's a privilege to have someone from the special operational forces in our midst," says Grandpa.

"Thank you, sir," says Randall Horton. "You are the reason I came. You, Mrs. Bennett, Glory Bea, and Lila June."

Mama's face turns the palest pink.

I scowl at my cards. Delilah was right. In the past few days, when Randall Horton wasn't with others, he's been here. He and Mama sat on the front porch swing in the cold and talked. I didn't know she had that many words in her. Mama and I missed our "hair rolling and playing Hearts" date last Saturday night. He better take off before it happens again.

"The Five & Dime had kites displayed in the window today," continues Randall Horton. "I took a chance and bought one for each of us. What do you say we fly them tomorrow afternoon?"

"Splendid!" says Grams.

"Perfect weather," says Grandpa.

"I have the day off," says Mama, and she looks at me. Hard.

I don't have an excuse and she knows it.

I say, "Yes," but inside I say, *No.*

At least Randall Horton only plays a few hands and leaves. Maybe to start packing his bag. Surely he's overstayed his welcome at the McGraths'.

We stand on the porch as he walks away. He stops at the picket fence and turns.

Grams, Grandpa, Mama, and I wave our two-handed Bennett good-bye. With our hands close to our faces, we swish them back and forth like windshield wipers, only faster. Apparently, I started this tradition when I was itty-bitty, and everyone in my family adopted it.

Do not, do not wave like us, Randall Horton.

"Thanks again," he calls.

Randall Horton returns our wave with two hands, *our* family wave, while I think, *Go away, go away, go away.*

Grams and Grandpa wander inside while Mama and I settle on the swing.

"Put your head on my lap," she says, and covers me with the afghan.

I lie on my side and rest my head on her dress. It is soft and warm.

"When is Randall Horton leaving, Mama?"

"Glory Bea, that kind of talk is not neighborly, especially since Mr. McGrath just offered him a job at the pharmacy."

I bolt straight up and focus on her face. Mama's eyes show disappointment. In me. I glare back.

"It wouldn't hurt you to be friendly, would it?"

It might.

"Randall's rented a room from the Crowleys," she says, "and will begin work next week."

"For how long?"

Mama looks skyward. "He wants to make a new start."

"What's wrong with New York?"

"Glory Bea Bennett! Everyone deserves a second chance at life."

"Will he be a soda jerk?" Having Randall Horton serve Ruby Jane or Grandpa and me our Dr Pepper floats might turn them sour.

Mama pinches her lips together. "Randall Horton is a pharmacist, like Mr. McGrath."

Good. At least he'll stay in the back of the store.

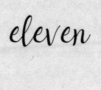

eleven

A: BEN is an expert on Mr. Drew Pearson. Plus B: Ruby Jane needs more than three words to say to him. Equals C: My friend should know more about Mr. Pearson.

So I'm off to the Gladiola library this morning because this afternoon I have to fly a kite. I'd take Ruby Jane but she's still out of town.

I skip to the front door, swing it open, and jump back. "Ben."

His hand is raised in a fist like he is just about to knock. "Uh . . . oh . . . hi," he stammers. "I've come to see your grandpa about the float."

"He's in his art studio."

Ever since Grandpa retired and started painting bluebonnets in the garage, he elevated the garage's name.

"Outstanding." Ben covers a yawn with his hand. "Thanks," he says, and takes off.

Wait. Why did I send him away? Forget the library. I grab my spiral notebook and barge into the studio, shouting out a question. Big stacks of newspapers line the walls.

Ben and Grandpa stop talking, and Ben turns over a piece of paper on the table real fast.

The scent of turpentine and oil paint wafts through the air. To me, it smells like happiness. I've taken only a few painting lessons from Grandpa, and he says, "Keep showing up and you'll improve."

"You want to know what?" Ben asks.

"Your favorite movie."

"What's your prediction?"

"Abbott and Costello Meet Frankenstein."

"Close," says Ben. "The greatest scene is where Costello gets hypnotized . . ."

Grandpa pulls his watch from his pocket and swings it back and forth. Ben lifts his arms out straight and walks stiff-legged around the studio like he is in a trance.

I snap my fingers in front of his face and he stops.

". . . and the doctor wants to put Costello's brain into the Monster."

I can think of someone who needs a new brain.

I've wondered if Daddy was captured and brainwashed, and that's why it's taking him so long to return.

"My top choice," says Ben, "is *The Story of G.I. Joe.*"

He holds up his two index fingers. *"Bup. Bup. Bup. Bup,"* he says, waving his hands back and forth like he is firing ammunition. *Tap. Tap. Tap. Tap.* "Ernie Pyle reports from the front lines," he says as his fingers rush over imaginary typewriter keys.

Ben sounds like a newsreel they show before a movie, complete with sound effects.

"Pyle was quite a guy," says Grandpa. "It's a shame we lost him."

I open my spiral and write down the titles.

"That looks official," says Ben, peering over my shoulder. He stifles another yawn.

I drop the notebook to my side and turn to look right into Ben's eyes. I am close enough to count all of his freckles. He flushes and looks at his shoes.

"Your favorite board game?" I ask, taking a step back. Ruby Jane loves Parcheesi.

Ben puts his hand under his dimpled chin.

It is not a hard question. I think I know his answer. Still, I want confirmation.

I poise my pencil over my notes and wait. The clock on the wall behind Grandpa's easel ticks loudly. Ben cracks his knuckles.

"Chess."

"Thank you," I say, and close my spiral.

Ben rubs his eyes.

"Everything okay?" I ask.

Ben exchanges a look with Grandpa. "My dad had a rough night."

Nightmares. Most times, Ben's daddy doesn't remember them. Except Ben and his mama do. Sometimes us neighbors do too. Mr. Truman's screams travel, but not as much in the winter when windows are closed.

I'm never sure what to say, so I say the only thing I can think of. "I'm sorry, Ben. Real sorry."

I don't think Ben knows what to say either, so he taps his fist against his heart.

"I'll see if he's up for a visit later today or tomorrow," says Grandpa.

"Thank you, sir," says Ben.

Grandpa thumps my spiral. "Looks like you are on a mission," he says, changing the subject.

"I am," I say.

Back in my room, I look toward the train station. I turn away, pick up Daddy's photo, and perch on my bed. "I can't wait for you to come home, Daddy. I know I need more proof that you'll arrive on Valentine's Day. But I have a feeling. A really good feeling. So I've decided to act like it's true until proven otherwise. You'll be the star of the parade. Afterward, we'll celebrate your return every single day for the rest of your life. I've already figured out a few things for us to do: Sing 'Happy Birthday' to you five times with five different carrot cakes to make up for your lost birthdays. Find you a real four-leaf clover. And have Mr. Wyatt print up a special edition of the *Gladiola Gazette* that tells your story. Forty-six days, Daddy—just forty-six more days."

twelve

MAMA MUST WORK at the insurance agency this afternoon on account of last-minute end-of-the-year business.

Grams has an "it's New Year's Eve tomorrow and my date canceled" emergency.

Grandpa is going to keep Ben's dad company.

I inquired about a snowstorm, rain, lightning, hurricane, flood, and tornado. Only Grandpa said, "It's almost twenty degrees above freezing with nice winds, strong enough to stir the leaves on the ground. Near perfect winter weather conditions. Now skedaddle."

Which is why Randall Horton and I are standing at the edge of a nearby open field with two diamond-shaped paper kites for my first ever kite-flying experience while the wind whips my hair into my face. And the faintest smell of cow pies fills my nostrils.

I hold my kite by the cross-sticks as Randall Horton explains and demonstrates the basics. "Keep your line short at first and your back to the wind . . ."

His kite soars, leading us to the middle of the field, where he brings it back down.

All I hear is the *flap-flap-flapp*ing of wind on paper.

"Your turn," says Randall Horton.

I toss my kite into the air.

It dives to the ground.

"Great attempt," he says. "Try again."

I'm ready to leave, but I know I'll hear it from Mama if I do.

The result is the same.

The third time it flutters, like it wants to fly.

Then it sputters. Crashes.

Snap.

I pick up the torn and splintered pieces and turn to Randall Horton. Before he sees me, his face registers regret.

"I'm sorry," I say.

I didn't ruin his kite on purpose.

"Don't worry, Glory Bea, accidents happen. You've been a good sport to come with me."

I cock my head.

"Your daddy talked about you every day."

My eyes widen. "He did?"

"Your first word was 'da-da,' your favorite game was hide-and-seek, and you loved to draw the sky. He was very proud of you."

I blink. Lots.

Randall Horton holds up his kite. "How about we fly this one together?"

I set my broken kite in the grass and take his.

"Did you know that when you fly a kite, you are fishing for angels?" Randall Horton asks.

In case he's right, I tell them what I want.

The kite flies so high, we run out of string.

thirteen

WE ALWAYS EAT black-eyed peas for luck on New Year's Day. At least that hasn't changed. Grams has a pot simmering on the stove for tomorrow.

"It is not the end of the world," says Grams to someone on the other end of the phone before we sit down to supper.

From the top stair, I see her draw a heart on the telephone pad.

"That's right," she says, penciling an arrow through the heart. "It's the beginning of a new one."

Grams writes something and ends the call. I am too far away to see so I take a peek on my way to the kitchen. There is a name under the heart, *Arthur Benjamin*.

I don't know who that man is; however, I do know one thing: his heart is in good hands.

Unlike Ruby Jane's.

I look down at my small palms and fingers. I haven't made any more progress.

Ruby Jane and Ben aren't any closer to a photo on my Wall of Fame.

I traipse into the kitchen. The red-and-white-checkered oil-cloth is set with four white dinner plates.

Randall Horton is not here tonight.

Yet he is. In the conversation.

"We should call Randall at midnight to wish him Happy New Year," Grams says.

I swing around. "We never stay up that late."

"New Year, new ways," says Grams.

I scowl.

"We're moving forward, Glory Bea," says Grams. "Not backward. Join us."

What about standing still? Waiting. Planning. Or, at least, slowing down. There's plenty of time to move forward when Daddy returns.

Grandpa reports that he talked to the secretary of the glee club, also known as his wife, today and put in a request for a song or two in French during the parade.

"'Blue Skies,'" I say. *"S'il vous plaît."*

It was the song Daddy woke me up with every morning. It will be the perfect song to welcome him back.

"That's one of my favorites too," says Grams. "I'll suggest it to Mr. McGrath."

"Will the Gerbera Daisies and Dudes perform?" asks Mama, who was a roller-skating Daisy when she was a senior in high school.

"Wouldn't be a parade without them," says Grandpa.

"Maybe I'll participate this year," she says.

Mama still has her uniform but she hasn't skated since Daddy left. "I don't know if that's a good idea," I say. "You might fall."

"If I do," says Mama, "I'll get right back up."

"That's the spirit," says Grams.

"We may not have as big a shindig as those folks in New York City or even Fort Worth," says Grandpa. "However, it won't be because we don't try."

I shake off Mama's idea. "It will be the best parade ever," I say, and rub my shamrock charm.

We listen to Fred Astaire on the record player in the parlor and wait for midnight. Mama strokes my hair as I lay my head in her lap. Grandpa sings along with "Steppin' Out with My Baby" and puffs smoke rings from his once-a-year cigar. Grams hums as she knits a light green baby blanket for the county hospital nursery.

The McGraths play a spirited game of checkers in the study. Mr. and Mrs. play one game every day of the year and keep score. This is the tiebreaker.

Riiiiing. Ring. Riiiiing.

Mama pops up so fast, I tumble to the floor.

She forgets to say sorry and rushes out of the room.

No one ever phones after nine o'clock. Miss Connie will be fired up, and not in a good way.

Grams clutches her heart and Grandpa smiles extra wide.

I stand and brush myself off. "It's probably a wrong number," I say.

"Probably not," says Grandpa as Mama races up the stairs.

Why doesn't she take the call downstairs? It's closer.

"Be right back," I say, and I tiptoe under the staircase.

"I can't believe you called," says Mama. The second phone perches on a stand in the hall just outside my grandparents' bedroom.

No telling how many people's ears, including Miss Connie's, are tuned in to this conversation. One more won't hurt.

I put my finger on the receiver on the hall phone and lift it off the hook.

". . . had everything to live for. You, Glory Bea." Randall Horton's voice is soft. "George was the best guy on the planet."

He is right about that.

"I'm not George. You know that, Lila June. Nevertheless, I'm hoping you will let me get to know you even better this next year."

A sharp intake of breath fills my ear and my phone falls.

Who gasped? Mama? Me?

The phone clunks against the wall, and my heart feels like it might up and burst.

"Hello, Gladiola, Texas," I hear Mama say, and Randall Horton chuckles.

I grab the phone and put it back up to my ear.

Click, goes a receiver. *Click. Click.*

"Guess we had company," says Randall Horton.

Mama laughs. "Randall, you make me feel like the luckiest person."

"Lila June, I am the luckiest."

I can't listen anymore. I hang up and walk back to the parlor.

The McGraths have joined Grams and Grandpa. All don paper hats and hold kazoos in their hands.

Mrs. McGrath is beaming. She must have won the game.

I plop onto the sofa between my grandparents, my arms tight across my chest.

"Have you made a New Year's resolution, Glory Bea?" asks Grandpa, and he sets a kazoo in my lap.

"I forgot."

"It's not too late." Grandpa looks at the clock on the mantel, surrounded by photos of my daddy. "You've got four more minutes."

I rub my shamrock and think. "Got it," I say, then blow my kazoo.

fourteen

I EAT TWO helpings of black-eyed peas today at noon.

One for me, and one for my daddy.

"Need any help packing?" asks Mama as she scooches over the clothes on my bed and sets down her small tan suitcase. Ruby Jane returned a few hours ago, and I'm headed to her house for the night.

"No thanks," I say.

A decal with GRAND CANYON in big letters is in the top left-hand corner of the suitcase. Mama and Daddy drove there on their honeymoon. To the right is a sticker of GALVESTON ISLAND written in cursive. I stand beside Mama and trace it with my hand.

"You picked it because you loved the fancy letters," she says, and taps my nose.

I still do. Like a sunset, the orange background in the letters blurs up to blue.

"Your daddy and I were going to travel the world together." Mama kisses the top of my head. "We didn't make it very far. But I bet you will."

I don't want to go anywhere. I want to stay right here. Until he comes home.

Mama smells like a rose garden in full bloom. Like the McGraths' roses, which spill out onto the sidewalk every spring and make people stop and smile. "Bon voyage," Mama says, and leaves.

I click the lock on either side of her suitcase, the one we shared the last time we took a trip. I rub my hands across the smooth rusty-colored inside and into the pockets.

Ouch.

I pull out my hand, open it, and look at the jagged slivers of white, tan, and pink shell from an angel wing. It's from the Galveston beach Mama and Daddy and I visited before he shipped out. The same beach where I tucked a brown-and-white-speckled cowrie with its hard shell into his pocket for good luck. The shell he took with him. The shell he said he'd bring back. This is a sign.

He will come back. I am counting on it. More than ever.

For some reason Daddy is hiding, just like he used to do when we'd play hide-and-seek. He'd tuck behind doors, under tables, and in closets. I'd always figure out where he was.

These days, he could be anywhere. Like in a sea of soldiers at a parade.

I pack my clothes, grab my spiral notebook, and place it inside too. Then I head downstairs. My clothes shift from side to side, trying to fill up the empty spaces.

The phone rings just as I am fixing to push open the kitchen door and say good-bye.

"I'll get it," I yell, and put down my suitcase.

It is Randall Horton.

"Hello, Glory Bea. May I please speak to your mother?"

"She can't come to the phone right now. Bye."

Technically what I said is true. She can't come if I don't call her.

I hang up and swing toward the kitchen.

The phone rings. Again.

"We must have gotten disconnected, Glory Bea. May I please leave a message?"

"Sure."

"Please tell your mother I'm running late and it'll be an hour before I pick her up."

"An hour," I say.

"Thank you very much."

"Bye."

Click.

"On my way," I tell Mama and Grams as I push open the kitchen door with my suitcase.

They are at the table sipping coffee. Mama's hair is now styled and sprayed.

"Have fun," says Grams. "Now come give me some sugar."

I kiss both of them good-bye.

"Glory Bea," says Mama. "Who was on the phone?"

"A stranger," I say.

I wave and skip out the door, swinging my suitcase.

fifteen

"A WAR MOVIE?" says Ruby Jane as we roller-skate side by side around the empty church parking lot next to her house. "He likes to sit in the middle of the theater? We are not at all alike."

"You don't need to agree with your boyfriend about everything. That would be boring."

Ruby Jane picks up speed. "Boyfriend? You said 'boyfriend.'" She points her toes out, spreads her arms wide, and glides across the blacktop. Her straighter-than-straight hair rises behind her. "I love that word."

I tell her what else I know.

Ruby Jane skates over with a frown. "Curly hair? Coca-Cola?"

"Don't worry," I say, putting a hand on her shoulder. "This just proves opposites attract." At least that's what I heard Grams say once.

As soon as we walk into her house, Homer runs up to us. "Why did the cow cross the train tracks?" He looks at his sister. "Don't tell."

Ruby Jane puts her fingers to her lips and pretends to zip her mouth.

"That's a hard one," I say. "You might have to help me out."

"To moooooooove to the other side."

"Homer," I say, removing his railroad cap and tousling his hair, "you should be on the radio."

"Ruby Jane, can I tell you something?" I say in a low voice once we've tucked ourselves into the twin beds across from each other and turned out the lights.

"Anything."

I flip over onto my side and prop my head up on my elbow to face her. She is lying on her back. I can't see well enough to know whether her eyes are open or not.

"You know how I've talked about my daddy coming back?"

"Uh-huh."

"Like maybe he'll show up on Christmas or the Fourth of July or my birthday?"

"I like the birthday story the best."

"And remember when I told you about that man in Tula who had amnesia and came home and how I thought maybe that's what happened to my daddy?"

"I remember."

"Well, I think I've figured out when he's coming."

Ruby Jane flings off her covers and leaps over to my bed. I sit up to make room.

"When?" she asks.

"I'm not one hundred and ten percent sure. Yet. Which is why I haven't said anything."

"That's okay. Tell me anyway."

"He's returning with the Merci boxcar."

"Seriously?"

"Yes. I think. I hope. And you know what else?"

"What?"

"I think it's coming on Valentine's Day."

"Oh, Glory Bea, you're going to make me cry." And she waves her hands in front of her face.

"It gets even better."

"No."

"Yes. Valentine's Day is my parents' anniversary."

"It's too good to be true," says Ruby Jane, falling back on my bed and bouncing right up. "Your story makes perfect sense. Or . . . absolutely no sense."

"What do you mean, no sense?"

Ruby Jane quiets. "What if he's gone for good?"

"Do NOT say that! I thought you were my best friend. I thought you believed in miracles."

"I want to believe, Glory Bea, I do. But . . ."

"This is when he's coming back. It has to be."

"Why?"

"Because there's a problem."

"What?"

"Not what. Who. Randall Horton. He is spending way too much time at my house. He took me kite flying the other day. Now he's going to live here." I grab my pillow and hug it extra tight. "I think Mama is forgetting my daddy."

"Uh-oh."

Ruby Jane doesn't say, *Don't worry about Randall Horton.* She doesn't say, *When your daddy comes, your mama won't even look at Randall Horton.* Ruby Jane doesn't say anything at all.

Except, "I'm sorry, Glory Bea." Then she moves back to her bed.

It was a mistake to tell her.

I pull my covers up to my chin, close my eyes, and try to brush away my doubts.

I beg for a miracle.

Something wakes me in the middle of the night. A sliver of moonlight shines into the room. Ruby Jane is still asleep. The murmuring rush of a train fills my ears. I listen until I can't hear it anymore.

sixteen

"TIMING IS ESSENTIAL," Grams says into the telephone as I hop down the stairs Friday afternoon, and then she hangs up.

"Glory Bea, I need one more thing from the store. As well as some fresh air. Let's take a trip to Mays Market."

In math, the shortest distance between two points is a straight line. Grams likes the longest.

"If we want to be back by dinner, we'd better start now," I say.

"That's my girl," says Grams, and she pulls on my ponytail.

We bundle up and make it to State Street in record time. We stay twenty minutes. Going there with Grams is like going to church. She has to howdy everybody before she can leave the premises.

I think we are leaving, when Mr. McGrath walks in. "Melba," he says, removing his hat, "just the person I wanted to see."

"At your service," says Grams.

"I found the sheet music to a song you suggested we sing during the parade."

"'Blue Skies'?" I ask.

Mr. McGrath taps his heel. "No, not that one. Besides, it will probably be a gray day like today."

I scrunch my face and barge into the cold. Only a few streaks of white interrupt the gray sky. I pull up my turtleneck sweater as high as it will go.

I stomp next to Grams as she moseys all the way down to the Gladiola Recreation Center, circles around the whole block, and, I hope, is finally heading home. Where I can slather lotion on my itchy, chapped face.

"Would you look at that," says Grams as she saunters up Mountain Laurel Lane.

A tan soft-sided bag rests a few feet away.

"It needs its owner, Glory Bea."

"I wonder whose it is?"

I bend down.

The second I touch the purse, it jerks away.

"Ah," I say, flinging my arms up like I am under arrest, while Grams jumps back.

"Hooyah!" shouts Ben as he springs from behind the bushes.

"You ought to be ashamed of yourself," I say. "Scaring me. Not to mention an old woman."

"How did you do that?" Grams asks.

"Fishing line," he answers, then grabs the purse and dangles it in the air to show her.

Grams nods. "Had any other takers?"

"You're my first."

"Don't change a thing," she says. "This brings back such memories. Glory Bea's daddy and your father pulled this same trick on me one time."

My daddy? Was once like Ben?

Before I fall asleep, I move to the window that faces town. On the roof of the train station, the light on top of the pole is green. The sky is cloudy, but the stars are surely still there. I leave the curtains open and turn to my daddy's picture.

I think about the upcoming blue-sky parade day. Mama and I will mill around the Gladiola Recreation Center with other folks until the starting time. Then someone with a high forehead, big smile, and twinkly eyes will come up behind me, put his hands over my eyes, and say, "Guess who?"

seventeen

MAMA IS in the kitchen when I get home from school. Blue flames dance below the teakettle on the cast-iron stove. Usually Mondays are busy at the insurance office; I guess Delilah's daddy let her off early.

Apron strings hang to her sides as she peels carrots and potatoes. She's chewed off all her lipstick on her bottom lip, and above her top lip are dots of perspiration. It is steamy in here. I take off my coat and cardigan.

Pots and pans and bowls cover the countertops. Pats of butter dot a chicken in the roasting pan on the kitchen table. Two stalks of broccoli from our garden stand in a pan of water.

I pluck an apple from the glass baking dish and toss it into the air.

Randall Horton is coming for dinner. Once he gets a taste

of Mama's cooking, he'll never come back. I guarantee it.

I take a bite of the apple.

"Glory Bea, that's for dessert."

"Sorry," I say. "Want some help?"

"Yes, you can cut the apples for the cobbler. Keep the skins on."

Grams always peels them first. Maybe Mama has a different recipe.

"Sure," I say. "Are we serving it à la mode?" It's French for "served with ice cream." Thanks, *Gladiola Gazette*. Last week Ruby Jane's mama taught us food vocabulary in her column. Words like *"café au lait"* (coffee with milk) and *"soupe du jour"* (soup of the day) and *"éclair"* (a pastry). If any of us ever get to France or a French restaurant, we'll be able to eat.

"Ice cream. I knew I'd forget something," says Mama as she transfers the vegetables to the roasting pan and sets it in the oven.

"Don't worry," I say. "This way the flavor won't be hidden."

She organizes all the ingredients for the dessert on the counter: two kinds of sugar, flour, salt, cinnamon, nutmeg, baking powder, and an egg.

"I'll ready the table while you finish with the apples," she says. She opens up the cabinet with the china we use only for holidays, takes a set of plates, and leaves through the swinging door.

I snatch the container of salt and dump a big old gob of it into the sugar canister.

Aha! and *Hmm* mix inside me.

Mama sails in and out a few more times.

"I'll be your recipe reader," I say when she returns for good. "First up, three quarters of a cup of white sugar."

Mama dips the measuring cup into the canister labeled FLOUR.

"Oh, silly me," she says, and corrects her error. "You'd think I've never cooked before."

"Next, two tablespoons brown sugar."

Mama follows all my instructions and, when she is done, crumples in a chair. "I think we're all set. This can go in the oven when the chicken comes out." She puts her hands on the table and pushes herself up. "Now I'm going to get ready."

I'm going to get ready too. For Daddy's return. I search for the hole punch, today's newspaper, and a grocery sack, and sprint upstairs. I will make enough confetti for my whole family to shower him with at the parade.

Eating dinner takes forever. Grandpa and Randall Horton have seconds. Grams gets a call, which we all overhear:

"I see," she says. "It was a New Year's Eve crush." Pause. "What do you say we pursue other possibilities?" Pause. "I can't promise true love by Valentine's Day. Love has its own timetable. We will, of course, hope for the best."

Finally, everyone picks up their dishes and takes them to the kitchen.

"This dessert smells divine," says Grams as Mama pulls the steamy cobbler from the oven and divides it into bowls.

We sit back down and Mama picks up her spoon. Randall Horton is the first to taste the dessert.

Mama watches as his eyes widen. He swallows.

"Nice and hot," he says, and picks up his coffee.

Mama takes a bite. "Oh no," she says, putting her napkin over her mouth. "It's too salty. I must have . . ."

She looks at me, lowers her napkin, and cocks her head.

I tighten the grip on my spoon and stare at my cobbler. She knows.

". . . I must have switched containers," she says, and my spoon clatters to the floor. "Please, don't anyone eat it."

"Well, now," Grams says after a bite. "I do believe you are right."

Mama closes her eyes. A giggle spurts out. And another.

This is like a trick Ben would cook up. She always laughs at his pranks.

"This meal will go down in his-toe-reee," sings Grams.

"Which is one of the reasons why I love this family," says Randall Horton.

I whip my head around.

"There's a lot not to love too," I say. "Mama can't cook, Grandpa hums off-key, Grams can talk your ear off, and, well, once I make up my mind, it's hard to change it."

"None of us is perfect, are we?" says Randall Horton.

eighteen

I CAN'T SLEEP.

I tiptoe downstairs and head for the canister of sugar. I take it to the trash can beside the back door and lift the canister lid. A note rests on top. *I love you, sugar. xx, Mama.*

I tuck it into the pocket of my bathrobe.

Back in the kitchen, I set the table for breakfast. I retrieve Mama's note and add to it: *I love you, too, Mama. xo, Glory Bea* and slip it under her cereal bowl.

A plate of brownies dusted with powdered sugar sits beside the refrigerator.

With a glass of cold milk in one hand, I grab the biggest brownie with my other and skulk toward the parlor. Just enough moonlight peeks through the windows to guide me.

Bong. Bong.

"Hush," I say to the grandfather clock.

I put the milk on the end table and settle into Daddy's leather chair. One bite of the brownie remains, and I nibble at it until it's gone. I wipe my hands on my bathrobe, turn on the lamp beside me, and reach for Mama's box of letters.

I've put my own letters from Daddy in a scrapbook that I've read fifty thousand times, though I've never read the ones he wrote just to Mama. When they arrived, she would read parts aloud to us, the parts that she said weren't mushy.

I open the wooden box, and letters spill onto my lap and the chair and onto the floor. Letters that aren't tied together with yellow ribbons like Daddy's. Letters that have block writing. Like an architect, Grandpa used to say.

Letters from Randall Horton. His Thanksgiving letters.

I pull at the collar of my nightgown, which is suddenly too tight. My throat goes dry and I try to swallow. My eyes move to the two envelopes on my lap. One is right side up, the other upside down. I brush them toward the floor.

I perch the wooden box on my lap and reach for the first bundle of letters. I untie the yellow ribbon, pick up the thin blue letter with its sharp creases, postmarked June 1, 1944, and read my daddy's last letter.

Dear Lila June,
I love you. You know that, don't you?
I love you more than life itself. I love our
beautiful daughter too.

*Things are really heating up over here.
We will succeed. I already taste victory. I
am proud to be a part of this—to make the
world a better place for our family. Good will
triumph over evil. Count on it.*

*I can't wait to come back home. I want to
hold you in my arms and never let you go,
treat Glory Bea to Dr Pepper floats, teach her
how to beat my dad at chess, snag the biggest
perch in the river, and awaken our daughter
every morning with a song, even if she
thinks she's too old now.*

*Lila June, you and Glory Bea are the best
things that have ever happened to me. Know
that I think about you every minute of every
day.*

I will come home. I promise.

Missing you.

Your loving husband,

George

I knew it. I knew he'd come home. He promised.

nineteen

I TOSS Randall Horton's letters into the trash.

twenty

"ACCORDING TO GRAMS," I say as Ruby Jane and I peer through the windows of Mays Market the next day after school, "it's important that one person doesn't do all the talking." I lay my hands on her shoulders. "You, my friend, earn an A-plus for that."

Ruby Jane's mouth opens so wide, I think I see her tonsils in her reflection.

"Everyone likes to be asked questions," I say, moving to her side. "They show interest and will give you something to say. You've nailed 'How are you?' Let's think up more."

Ruby Jane squints into the window. Delilah heads the line of kids at the cash register for candy, pop, or a pickle. She waves her baton at us. We wave back.

"You don't think Delilah and Ben—" begins Ruby Jane.

"I think," I say, nudging her side, "that we should concentrate on you. What is something you really want to ask him?"

Ruby Jane brightens. "Do you like me?"

I cover my ears. "You *could* say that. Only, you might want to build up to it instead. What about some not-so-serious questions first?"

"Like?"

"Like 'What's the best trick you've ever pulled?' Or 'Besides Drew Pearson, who would you invite to dinner and why?' Or 'Would you rather eat a barrel of jalapeños or a barrel of pickles?'"

"I've never heard of a barrel of jalapeños."

I whistle the air out of my lungs. "Me either. Tell you what? Let's practice. I'll be Ben. Say hi."

She does. Megaphone loud.

As Ben I say, "Hi. How's it going?"

"GOOD."

Silence.

"It's still your turn, Ruby Jane."

"I know," she whispers.

"Try a question I suggested."

"Tell me what some are again?"

"Don't worry. Go with 'What's new with you?' instead."

Ruby Jane's big voice returns and her body is as rigid as a railroad track.

As Ben I say, "Mr. Bennett and I have teamed up to work on a float for the parade. What's new with you?"

"NOT MUCH."

"In future conversations, you could expand your answer."

"Okay."

Delilah flits out of the store with an open bag of M&M's. She pops a yellow candy into her mouth and says, "I have news."

"Do tell," I say. Of course I know she will whether we ask or not.

"Ben and I are on the ballot for king and queen of the Valentine's Dance."

Ruby Jane grabs my arm. "That's fantastic," I say. For Delilah.

"Toodle-oo," she says, and twirls her baton down the street.

"Pretend that never happened," I say to Ruby Jane, though I know she won't.

"Here are your two assignments: one, memorize and practice 'What's new with you?'; and two, add, 'What's your latest prediction?'"

"All right."

"After you've actually asked them, I'll give you more."

Baby steps. Not leaps. Not yet.

Did You Know?
Gladiola Gazette
January 12, 1949

It is my quest to continue to marinate
us in all things French before the
Texas Merci Train boxcar arrives.
Well, dear readers, it will be here in
approximately one month! Why, that's
only a few issues away. So, in order
to accelerate our learning of French,
like last week's column, today's column
is devoted entirely to this Romance
language. Never fear. Remember, you
know more than you think you do. And to
prove it, here are a dozen more French
words you use all the time, or may use
at least some of the time:

  Adieu (farewell)
  Armoire (wardrobe)
  Ballet (dance)
  Brunette (brown-haired woman)
  Bureau (office, desk)
  Chauffeur (driver)
  Chic (stylish)
  Extraordinaire (extraordinary)

ANNE BUSTARD

    Fiancé (betrothed)
    Silhouette (figure, outline of a person)
    Souvenir (a keepsake)
    Unique (one of a kind)
    So now you know, dear Gladies, now you
know,

    Penny Pfluger

twenty-one

I WAS RIGHT to throw away Randall Horton's letters. Mama doesn't miss them. Almost two weeks have passed and she hasn't said a thing.

Mama's not even opened the box. I would know. I moved it to a different shelf and tied the yellow ribbon in a new way.

Even though I've about memorized all the letters Daddy wrote to me, I'm rereading one every night until he comes.

This morning, Mama thanked me three times for the Saturday breakfast I made just for her. I delivered cereal and milk, buttered toast with marmalade, orange juice, coffee with extra sugar, and the newspaper on a big tray.

"What's the special occasion?" she asked as I fluffed the bed pillows behind her.

"You're special every day," I said. "And sometimes I forget to tell you."

I don't say that even though I'm glad I got rid of your letters, I feel guilty, and this is how I'm making amends.

How to handle a resistant client? With firmness and sweetness.

"Think of this as an investment in your future," I say to Ruby Jane as we enter the public library later that morning.

"I already know lots of things Ben likes," she says, and tucks her hair behind her ears. "What good has that done?"

Not much.

Their relationship has stalled. Ruby Jane's attempts to ask questions the past week and a half have failed. She hasn't gotten beyond hollering, "HI, HOW ARE YOU?" even though we practiced.

Maybe questions are too hard. Maybe current events is the answer.

"The more you have to talk about, the better. So today you're going to read some Drew Pearson columns."

"Why can't I just listen to him on the radio?"

"You can. You should. His show is only once a week. As in tomorrow. And we're going to see Ben at the soda fountain after the movie today."

"This sounds too much like homework. I like it better when you just tell me stuff."

"Come on," I say, and steer her to an empty table.

I grab the last few editions of the Austin paper, take off my coat, and sit beside my friend. The library is toasty, yet Ruby

Jane still wears her coat buttoned up to her chin.

"Start reading," I say, and pull the chain on the table light.

Ruby Jane sighs, props her elbows on the table, and peers over the pages. Her hair falls forward and covers her cheeks. "I hope this doesn't take too long."

Before we leave, I check out a book on how to play chess. Why not get a jump start on lessons with Daddy?

It's my turn to pick, but the entire back row at the theater is taken. So Ruby Jane and I take her favorite seats in the front row. Center. The chairs on either side of us are empty. I put my soda cup on the floor beside me, and Ruby Jane holds the popcorn perched on the armrest between us. She shouldn't eat it because of her braces, though that hasn't ever stopped her. As the red velvet curtains part, I sink into my seat and count down the numbers that flicker before me.

Images of a harbor fill the screen as a crane lifts a boxcar onto the deck of a gigantic ship. The words THANK YOU, AMERICA, flash in the center.

I sit up with a start, knocking over the popcorn, and tilt forward.

"Le Havre, France," the voice-over begins, and I grab Ruby Jane's arm.

My eyes dart over the images, trying to take them all in. It is too much, too fast. I want the camera to slow down, slow down so that I can see everything. The voice explains that the ship is named *Magellan*. A crowd on the dock watches the boxcar swing from the crane, and the camera zooms in. Men and women in overcoats stand nearby. One wears a US Army coat. His image blips by for just a second. I know—I know that smile.

I squeeze Ruby Jane's arm and she squeezes back.

"It's him," I say.

"Maybe," says Ruby Jane.

I knew she'd believe.

I rewind the image in my head. He is the right height. He is the right age. Most importantly, he has the right smile.

I let go of Ruby Jane's arm and fall back in my chair.

He will board that ship. He will travel with the train. He will keep his promise. Now I am one hundred and ten percent sure.

"We're not leaving," Ruby Jane and I tell the usherette, also known as Irma, after the movie. We stick to our seats like chewing gum.

"We want to see the newsreel again," says Ruby Jane.

"You know the rules," says Irma. "You have to leave."

"This is an extra-special emergency," says Ruby Jane.

"Talk to the boss," says Irma.

"Where is he?" she asks.

"Front office."

Mr. Pfluger sits behind an enormous wooden desk covered with papers. Autographed photos of Bob Hope, Bing Crosby, and Ingrid Bergman smile over his shoulders.

"We need a favor, Mr. Pfluger," I say.

He barely looks up. "Ruby Jane, you may not have an extension on your allowance. I've already given you three."

"Daddy, you haven't even let us ask yet."

Ruby Jane puts her hands behind her back and crosses her fingers. I grasp my charm bracelet.

"We'd like a private screening of the newsreel," she says.

Why didn't I think of that?

"That's not possible," says Mr. Pfluger, meeting our eyes. "We are on a very tight schedule."

"In that case, we'd like to see it again at the four o'clock showing," pushes Ruby Jane.

"That you can do," says Mr. Pfluger. "If you pay."

"Daddy. Then we won't have enough money for our float."

"Is that so?" he says. "Now, please, I have paperwork to finish." And as if to make his point, he waves a stack of paper at us.

"Glory Bea, I think we should spend our money on more movie tickets instead of at the soda fountain," Ruby Jane says as we leave.

"What about Ben?"

"I'll see him at school on Monday."

This is why Ruby Jane is my best friend.

We watch the newsreel from the first row center, again. In twenty-three days, I will see that smile and his twinkly eyes in person.

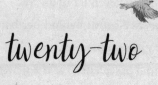

twenty-two

RUBY JANE was wrong about seeing Ben on Monday. Or Tuesday. Or any other day this past week. He was out with the flu.

I flop onto my bed Sunday afternoon. My empty Wall of Fame is in the shadows. What else can I do? Grams says everyone appreciates extra effort. The Pearson facts qualify.

Then I know. It's so obvious, I can't believe I didn't think of it before.

A few minutes later, Ruby Jane is in my kitchen. "Love is about taking risks," I say.

"Why do I think this is going to be bad?" Ruby Jane twists a strand of her straight copper-colored bangs.

"Ben likes curly hair, remember?"

"Are you sure you can do this?"

"Positive. I've helped Grams with lots of her perms." Then I pull out a chair and tell her, "Sit right here." I put two towels around her shoulders, comb out her two short braids, and get to work.

It is simple, really. I take small sections of Ruby Jane's hair, cover the end of each with white tissue paper, and wind them around and around and around a plastic roller. She only says "ouch" a few times. I ignore her headache.

Then I shake the bottle of solution from Grams's stash. "Hold the towel to your forehead and close your eyes and nose. Here comes the stink."

"You think Ben will notice?"

"One hundred percent guaranteed."

I turn the bottle of milky white liquid upside down and soak each roller.

"It's cold," she says as a stray line of liquid runs down her neck.

"Sorry," I say.

My eyes smart from the ammonia. I breathe through my nose, and when I can't abide the smell any longer, I open the back door and let in the freezing air.

"Now," I say, setting the timer. "We wait."

Grandpa wanders in for pie. He must be hungry, because he stays in spite of the aroma. "I've got additional information on the Merci boxcar," he says as he plates a slice of delectable buttermilk pie. "The Texas committee has finalized its arrival date."

I exchange looks with Ruby Jane. "I thought it was Valentine's Day."

"Almost," says Grandpa. "February sixteenth."

I catch my frown in the middle and reverse it. "Close enough," I say.

Two extra days. I can wait two extra days.

Because two days after that, Daddy will sing "Happy Birthday" to me!

He might even bring me a gift from France, though of course Daddy will be enough of a gift.

"Good luck, girls," says Grandpa, and leaves.

"Oh, Ruby Jane, you look adorable," says Grams, handing her a mirror when we're finished.

Ben will notice, all right. Tight ringlets boing around her face. "Gladiola's very own Shirley Temple," says Grams.

"When she was four," says Ruby Jane, scowling at her image.

"Think Shirley Temple and Cary Grant last year," I say. They were in a romantic comedy that Ruby Jane loved. I point to my chin. Cary Grant has a chin dimple like Ben.

My friend smiles just enough to show some of her top braces.

"This is the most perfect setup," I say. I put a hand behind my neck, poof one side of my hair, and strike a Hollywood pose. "Do this."

Ruby Jane obeys.

"Look at you," I say.

"I am," she says, glowering. She holds the mirror out to Grams. "How am I going to go out in public like this?"

"With a smile?" asks Grams.

"I'm leaving," says Ruby Jane, standing.

She grabs her coat and puts it over her head.

"Remember to listen to Drew Pearson tonight," I say as she rushes out the door.

"Change takes getting used to," adds Grams.

The back door flings open and Ruby Jane whips her head around the doorframe. "You're fired, Glory Bea." And she slams it shut.

I wince.

"What was that all about?" asks Grams.

"Nothing." Everything.

"I'll help you tidy up," says Grams. "Then I've got a phone call to make."

The stinky-burn-your-eyes ammonia smell still lingers, even when we're done cleaning, reminding me that I hurt my best friend. I can't seem to warm up. Even with an extra sweater.

I sit on the staircase just out of Grams's view while she picks up the receiver. Only, she doesn't make a call. Not really.

"How do you feel about a pet pig?" she asks Miss Connie.

Of course I can't hear her answer. "He's a stamp collector

too," says Grams. "Blueberry pie is his favorite."

Afterward, I ask Miss Connie to make a call.

I touch the pushpin that Grandpa moved on the map of the world beside me. It is almost to the middle of the Atlantic Ocean. *Hurry up, Daddy.*

"Woof, woof."

"Hi, Homer. May I speak to Ruby Jane?"

"She stinks."

I take a deep breath. "Will you tell her it's me?"

The phone clunks down and I hear steps walk away.

"Poodlehead," he yells. "Telephone."

A door bangs and footsteps race back to the phone. "She doesn't want to talk to you. But I do. What did the caboose say to the first car?"

"Hmmmm."

"Don't leave me behind."

Miss Connie giggles.

I don't.

How I hope Ruby Jane will feel different soon.

Later, as I try to fall asleep, I realize I forgot to keep my New Year's resolution today—to do one thing every day to make Daddy's homecoming the best ever. I must redouble my efforts tomorrow.

twenty-three

FORGIVENESS. That's what I want.

I seek out Ruby Jane before school the next morning. A pink-and-white scarf covers her head. Tight curls of orangish-brown boing below the scarf line as she and Delilah move swiftly down the hall.

"I'm sorry, Ruby Jane," I say as I catch up to my friend. "Very, very sorry."

"She isn't talking to you," says Delilah, and she shakes her silver baton at me. Ruby Jane stares straight ahead. No sign of her braces.

This is worse than I imagined. Not only is my best friend still mad at me; she likes my least favorite person better.

"I tried to call."

"She couldn't come to the phone," says Delilah as we zip past the office. "She was too busy washing her hair trying to undo the damage. More than seven times, she told me. In fact, I think it was ten."

"Oh, Ruby Jane."

"I asked her if you'd tested a strand of her hair first," says Delilah.

We all know the answer to that—no.

Delilah rattles on about the perm directions that come inside every box.

Directions I've never read.

"Everyone's looking at me," whisper-yells Ruby Jane, turning toward me. "For the wrong reason. Now I can't bring myself to see you-know-who."

"Will you forgive me? Please. I thought it would work. I'll do anything to make it up to you."

Ruby Jane stops. Her eyes brighten and she points to the red-and-white banner hanging above the trophy case.

"I want to go to the Valentine's Day Dance with Ben." She smiles bigger than big and taps the middle of her chin.

What?

And Delilah looks pleased?

A Dr Pepper float, a movie ticket, a magazine, something like that. Something possible.

Instead, Ruby Jane has asked for the impossible.

Valentine's Day is two weeks from today.

"Delilah's going with Harry Ackerman," says Ruby Jane.

Delilah bobs her head. "We could double-date," she squeals.

"Oh! And whoa!" I say.

"And your answer is . . . ?" asks Delilah as she twirls her baton.

"I'll try. I promise."

Delilah stops midtwirl. "Not good enough," she says, and tosses her hair.

"I mean, what a great idea."

Satisfied, they speed away.

That afternoon, the mayor's wife is in the parlor with Mama while Grams and I listen in from the foyer.

". . . because your George served in France, Mr. Crowley and I insist that you and Glory Bea have a special place in the parade. We'd like the two of you to ride in a car."

Say yes, Mama.

"We'd love to, Mrs. Crowley. Thank you very much."

Grams folds her hands together and I bounce in place.

As we move into the study, I say, "Since his dad's return from the hospital, Ben hasn't been at dinner. We should ask him over tomorrow night. I'll invite Ruby Jane and we'll add a leaf to the table."

"Brilliant," says Grams. "Just brilliant."

That is a high compliment. "Thanks. There's no need to ask Randall Horton, is there?"

Grams studies me. "I will check with your mama. Now, would you like to extend the invitations, or shall I?"

"Be my guest."

✳ ✳ ✳

Ben accepts.

Ruby Jane calls me three minutes later. "I don't know how you did it, Glory Bea. You are the best."

I've been forgiven. At least for now.

"Remember Drew Pearson."

"Okay. Sure."

I pray the third invitee will turn down Grams.

I borrow Grandpa's shoe polish, sneak into Mama's closet, and shine Daddy's shoes. The insides are a touch moldy. I'm sure there's a fix for that.

Then I zoom down to Grandpa's studio and knock.

Grandpa opens the door with a smile. "What can I do you for, Glory Bea?" The stacks of newspapers have grown up to the windowsills and beyond.

"I'd like to paint, please."

"Take your pick," says Grandpa, motioning to the half-dozen prepped white canvases on the plywood table. An assortment of paintbrushes protrudes from an old glass jar nearby.

"*Merci beaucoup*," I say, and set up my easel and tubes of paints.

I'm new to oils. Crayons and watercolors have been my mediums until last month. Mama's collected her favorites in an album in the study.

I squeeze the color onto my wooden palette, add oil to thin it, and dip my brush into the now muted blue.

Unlike Grandpa, I will not paint a scene of bluebonnets.

It doesn't take me long to cover the spiral-size canvas with a light undercoat. Tomorrow it'll be dry enough to add thick swaths of vibrant blues.

As I wipe the paint from my hand, Grandpa asks, "Do you already have a name for it?" He likes to title his paintings. Sometimes I help.

"*Blue Skies*," I say.

It's a painting for my daddy about his favorite kind of day.

twenty-four

I FINISH Daddy's painting the next afternoon. Cerulean, turquoise, and cobalt blues, with touches of white, stain my hands, but I leave them be. To remember.

Grams stands next to the stove and ladles the juice from the pan over the platter of pot roast. Usually it's a Sunday meal, except tonight we've got company.

"Are you going to the Valentine's Day Dance?" Ben asks me as he picks up a bowl of peas.

"Uh-huh," I say, and head for the swinging door with the mashed potatoes. *And you, Ben Truman, are going with Ruby Jane.*

I push the door with my elbow and stop. Only, Ben doesn't. Something hard jabs me in the side. "Oh no!" I say.

"Sorr—" says Ben.

In the dining room, everyone stands behind their chairs.

Randall Horton is behind my daddy's. The chair with a message I wrote in crayon on its underside after he left. No one has sat in that chair except Daddy. No one.

Randall Horton's hands clutch the top of the sculpted wooden frame.

Ruby Jane's mouth is open and no words come out.

"Everything's a-okay, Glory Bea," says Grandpa, and waves me in.

I glower at Mama. Only, she doesn't look at me. We added an extra leaf to the table, and she set it. Eight chairs. Seven people. Seven settings. Her head is bowed as she tosses the salad. Why didn't someone else say something? Why doesn't someone tell him to move?

"You all are blocking traffic," says Grams from behind.

"I'll keep the door open," I say, and let Ben and Grams pass by.

"Mercy," Grams says, and stops. Everyone turns toward her. "Randall," she says softly, "it's been a long time since anyone sat in that chair beside me."

Randall Horton looks at the vacant place setting to his right, where Mama should have sat him. He pinches the top of his nose and takes a deep breath. Then he taps the chair with his fist. "George is—George is irreplaceable."

"You can say that again," I say, glaring at Randall Horton.

"Glory Bea!" says Mama. Or did she say, "Glory be"?

The look on her face makes it clear she said my name. All eyes glance at me and then to the table Mama set.

When my daddy comes back, Randall Horton will vanish.

Grandpa clears his throat. "We're happy to have you, Randall," he says. "Happy to have all of y'all." He pulls out Grams's chair, and everyone begins to sit.

"Join us, won't you, Glory Bea?" asks Grandpa.

"Please," says Mama.

My paint-splashed hands are on fire. The handles on the serving dish are too hot and I can't hold on any longer. I rush to the empty space between Randall Horton and me and set it down.

"Here you go," says Ben, and pulls out my chair.

Grandpa says grace and we pass the food around the table.

This dinner is supposed to be about Ruby Jane and Ben. Randall Horton is not about to ruin it.

"Ruby Jane's starting her junior first-aid certificate this Saturday," I say, and pick up the peas. "Her instructor said, 'Ruby Jane will be a lifesaver.'"

My friend adjusts her neck scarf. She smiles too; only, her upper lip snags on her braces. She quickly recovers. I don't think anyone—and by "anyone," I mean Ben—noticed.

"Are you thinking of a career in medicine?" asks Randall Horton.

"Maybe," says Ruby Jane, and she takes the bowl of potatoes from Ben. No eye contact.

She said a word! And she didn't shout. I'll take victories, no matter how small.

"Ruby Jane is very interested in Drew Pearson these days," I say. Ben hands her the platter of pot roast. Ruby Jane holds one end and he holds the other. Their eyes meet.

I cover my smile with my hand as my soon-to-be Wall of Famers grin at each other.

"He thinks the government may have to buy up a lot of grain from the farmers this year," says Ben.

"Yes," says Ruby Jane as she forks a piece of pot roast onto her plate. "Up to eight hundred million bushels, and I predict that number will increase."

I am so proud of Ruby Jane that I actually clap.

"Hear, hear," says Grandpa, and joins in.

After everyone has left, Ben and I stack the dishes on the sideboard. "What's your favorite movie, Glory Bea? What board game do you like to play the most? Where do you sit in the movies?"

Before I can answer, Grams sweeps into the kitchen.

"Love is in the air," she says. *"Oui?"*

ANNE BUSTARD

Did You Know?
Gladiola Gazette
February 2, 1948

If you haven't heard about the Merci
Train, you've been living under a rock.
Or are not a regular reader of my
column. Any who, today, dear readers,
the boxcars will dock in Weehawken, New
Jersey, just across from New York City!
Which means the Texas boxcar will pay
us a visit before we know it! I have it
on good authority that the floats for
the parade are coming along splendidly,
the decoration committee is ready to
paint our town red, white, and blue—
or should I say blue, white, and red,
the colors of the French flag—and the
Gladiola Glee Club is in fine form, as
are the bands and marchers.

Mayor Crowley has confirmed the Texas
boxcar's arrival date.

Consider this your official invitation!
WHO: Everyone
WHAT: The Texas Merci boxcar's stop in
Gladiola, Texas

WHERE: Parade downtown, speeches at
the train station, and a Bar-B-Que potluck
immediately following at Gladiola Primary
and Intermediate

WHEN: 9:00 a.m., February 16, 1949, and
beyond

I am not at liberty to reveal the
special surprise, but be advised, there
will be one, or perhaps I should say—
someone!

Jusque-là, which means, "until then."

À bientôt! See you soon!

So now you know, dear Gladies, now you
know,

Penny Pfluger

twenty-five

"HELLO, KING. Hello, Queen. Hello, Bishops, Knights, Rooks, and Pawns."

I touch each piece on the chessboard late Saturday morning. Ruby Jane is still at her first-aid class, so it's me and *The Game of Chess* book.

Only, it isn't for beginners, and I'm at a loss.

Wilson barks at the front door and I happily say good-bye to the occupants of the chessboard.

Ben's come looking for my grandpa, so I follow them to the studio.

I'm after one thing.

The windows are covered with newspaper—which Grandpa does in the winter to keep out the cold. Only a few days ago, it unexpectedly warmed again.

I spot a sign on the door: NO ADMITTANCE.

"Sorry," says Ben. "Entrance denied."

"Excuse me?"

Grandpa opens the door just enough for a whiff of our painting supplies to escape.

Ben and Wilson slip inside.

I do an about-face, march into the kitchen, grab a bottle from under the sink and the binoculars, and get to work.

A few minutes later, I pound on the studio door.

Ben cracks it open. "Yes?"

"You know that raccoon you saw in the live oak when you did the bird report a while back? He's returned."

I hand Ben the binoculars. He steps outside and quickly closes the door, but not before Wilson scampers out. I point at the tree in the far corner. "Look halfway up."

Ben fixes the glasses to his eyes and moves his head up and down and all around. "I don't see him," he says, and lowers the binoculars.

"Funny," I say. "I'm looking right at him."

Wilson barks and wags his shaggy white-tipped tail.

Black rings Ben's eyes.

Ben touches his face, smearing the shoe polish. He rubs his fingers together and laughs. Long and loud. "Permission to copy."

"Only if you stop tricking me," I say. "The straw episode, flashlight, purse . . ."

Grandpa emerges from the studio.

"Bravo, Glory Bea," he says. "However, if you think this is going to get you inside our workshop, you're going to be sorely disappointed. The float is top secret."

I cross my arms.

"You could paint en plein air."

"Outside? No, thanks." It's not that warm today. Besides, I came for another reason. "May I have my painting, please?" It'll be good and dry by now.

Grandpa returns in a blink.

"Thanks."

Ben catches a flash of blue as I flip it over. "Top secret," I say.

I hug Wilson and then march off.

"See you later, Glory Bea," calls Ben.

I wave behind me and keep going.

twenty-six

GRAMS BELIEVES in practice.

So I stand next to her at the piano and turn pages while she plays and memorizes the words to her music for the parade. And receives love calls. In the middle of "La Marseillaise," the French national anthem, comes the familiar *Riiiiing. Ring. Riiiiing.*

"*Salut*, Glory Bea," says Miss Connie when I answer. "I just checked my numbers, and if your grandmother gets two more callers today, she'll break the all-time weekend record a day early."

One ring comes during "The Yankee Doodle Boy," and the record breaker while Grams sings "God Bless America."

"Well, now," says Grams, sitting back down on the piano bench and playing the first few bars of "Here Comes the Bride."

"I do believe my fortieth match may be just around the corner."

Eavesdropping on her matchmaking conversations, while beneficial, has gotten me only so far. There's an expert in my house and I need help. Ruby Jane had a breakthrough at dinner this week. I must build on the momentum.

"Grams, what are your favorite matchmaker tips?"

"I tell all my clients three things: be you, have fun, be positive."

That explains my challenge.

Since the February weather has improved, when Ruby Jane finally pops over after her class, we sit on the front porch swing. A shrub behind us doesn't know winter isn't finished, so its delicate yellow blossoms perfume the air, like honeysuckle.

We review the dinner with Ben. Twice. We've done so every day since Wednesday. And then how she felt about it. And whether or not she should have said anything different. Or worn anything different. Neither of us mentions her hair, though I really like her now-soft waves.

"In your professional opinion," asks Ruby Jane, perched on the edge of the swing with her feet grounded on the porch, "do you think Ben likes me?"

I join her on the edge of the swing, and we back it up as high as our tiptoes allow. "How could he not like you?" I say. "You're adorable."

"I think Ben likes you more."

"Don't be silly. We're like brother and sister."

"If you say so."

"That's exactly what I say. Look, I consulted Grams today and—"

"You mean you haven't before? I thought I'd hired a professional."

I ignore that question and pass on Grams's advice. "Let's work on number three, Ruby Jane—be positive."

"Double date, here I come!" she squeals.

"Right," I say. I need to stay positive too.

We hop back on, lift our shoes in the air, and let the swing propel us forward.

"Now about the Merci boxcar," I say. "In case you were wondering, I wanted you to know that I'm okay with the change in its arrival date."

Ruby Jane tilts her head as we rock back and forth. "I am too. It means two party days in a week."

"I still would have preferred Valentine's Day," I say. "Though, any day my daddy comes home is fine by me."

Ruby Jane's shoes brush the porch, and the swing jerks back and forth.

I grab the armrest so I won't topple off.

"He's halfway here now. I imagine that he's remembering his last days in France—going to museums in Paris, taking pictures of the Eiffel Tower, and eating escargot, because he certainly won't be getting any around here. And of course, he's thinking about Gladiola. I made a 'Welcome Home' poster just for him before you came over," I say.

Ruby Jane stops the swing and pats my shoulder.

"What do you think?" I ask.

"Your story is better than a movie."

Yep, I am on the right track.

twenty-seven

MAMA IS LATE for breakfast. Two hours late. For the second day in a row.

I'm keeping count, and last night makes twice that she's missed our Saturday hair rolling and Hearts game.

I jiggle my leg under the red-and-white-checkered kitchen tablecloth, with my eyes on the clock. My lucky charm sways back and forth.

We've eaten without her. I've read the Sunday Austin newspaper, and Grams helped me finish my homework. I even made more confetti for us to shower Daddy with when he arrives. Now the bag is fuller than full.

"Good morning, everyone," Mama says as she prances into the kitchen and gives me a kiss on my head.

Her pink dress swishes and her hair is swept into a fancy French twist.

I raise my eyebrows. Grandpa eyes the clock. Grams beams.

"Sleep well?" asks Grams.

"Eight whole hours," says Mama.

"Were you up late studying French?" I ask.

"No, Randall and I just can't seem to stop talking."

Grandpa winks at Grams.

"A one a.m. bedtime isn't healthy," I say.

The clock ticks extra loud and Grams clears her throat. "How about some French toast, darling?"

"Have I told you how much I love you today, sugar?" says Mama, opening her arms wide.

"I have to get ready for church," I say, and leave.

I stop in front of the world map in the hall. According to the pushpins, the Merci Train boxcars on the Southern route are on the move first thing tomorrow. The New England and the Western routes will follow. I tap the tips of all the pins and bolt up the stairs.

On our way home from Grams's extra glee club practice that afternoon, I tell her, "All y'all sounded especially good today."

"It's all about blending in, Glory Bea. Unless it's a solo, we should sing as one voice."

Winter has returned, and I wrap and tuck the ends of my wool scarf around my neck. I forgot my gloves. "Some of Mr. McGrath's song choices for the parade . . ." I shake my head.

"I know you're disappointed he didn't honor your request."

I skip my hand across the top of a picket fence, turn, and stop. A small sliver is wedged into my pointer finger. "He is not one of my favorite people right now."

"No matter how much you don't like someone," says Grams, "you can always discover one thing about them to appreciate."

"Like what?" I say, ignoring the pain in my finger.

"His voice, his earnestness, his dedication to this community."

"I guess." I try to extract the splinter.

"Nobody's perfect, Glory Bea. Even you."

My daddy is perfect. His own mama should know.

"Give Randall Horton a chance," says Grams.

I look straight into her eyes. "We were talking about Mr. McGrath."

"Were we, now?"

I clasp the splinter between my fingernails and tug. It breaks under my skin.

I shove my hands into my pockets and fall two steps behind her in silence.

twenty-eight

VALENTINE'S DAY is one week away.

"Sorry I'm late," I say as I scoot in across the table from Ruby Jane and Delilah at lunch. Delilah pushes her baton that was saving me the space toward their side. Above us, red and pink paper hearts spin on the ends of strings from the cafeteria ceiling.

Ruby Jane surveys the sugar feast before her: an éclair, a vanilla frosted cupcake, a bag of penny candies, and a giant piece of fudge. I haven't seen Ruby Jane with that many sweets since last July, when Homer came home from a two-week stay with their grandparents; Freddy Sinclair, her then heartthrob, moved to Oklahoma City; and her swim party was rained out—all on the same day.

Specs of chocolate are embedded in her front braces.

"What's wrong?" I ask.

"Ruby Jane can't take it anymore," says Delilah, and she rolls her baton back and forth with her fingertips.

"Take what?"

Delilah's lifts her baton and points one end at me. "Is she going to the dance with Ben? Yes or no?"

"There's always hope. Be positive, remember?"

Ruby Jane picks up the vanilla cupcake. "Sometimes dreams don't come true," she says, and she nods to the next table.

Ben sits next to Claire Armstrong. She laughs at something he says.

Ruby Jane takes a bite through half her cupcake.

"She's new," I say. "He's friendly."

"He played softball with Claire and her brother all afternoon yesterday," says Delilah, clutching her baton. "Then had dinner at their house."

"I'm sure there's a logical explanation," I say. "Do not be discouraged, Ruby Jane."

"I agree," says Delilah.

In another bite, Ruby Jane's cupcake disappears. For the rest of lunch, my friend can't seem to get enough sugar.

"I appreciate all you've done, Glory Bea. Really, I do. And your encouragement too, Delilah," she says as we leave the cafeteria. "It's time for me to quit."

"No, you can't," I say.

Delilah turns her palms up and makes a don't-ask-me face.

Ruby Jane doesn't smile or say "okay."

I know she'll change her mind.

Mrs. Crowley's car is parked outside our house. Again. Two visits in three weeks? She is becoming a downright regular. Especially because I can't remember the last time either she or Mr. Crowley came over.

I open the front door real quiet. Mrs. Crowley's voice rings out from the parlor. I stack my schoolbooks and lunch box on the table next to the lilies and tiptoe closer. I press my head next to the wall to listen.

". . . are so very happy for you and your new relationship with Randall."

I clamp my hands over my mouth.

"When it's appropriate, Mr. Crowley and I would like to host a party in your honor. You will make a beautiful bride."

"Mrs. Crowley! You are making a grand assumption."

"Give it some thought, my dear."

I back up and ease through the front door.

Wham.

I slam it shut and run.

Run past Ben coming up our walk. Run as fast as I can down my street.

Mama? Remarried?

No.

Never.

twenty-nine

BEEP! BEEEEEP!

A car jerks to a stop as I fly across the intersection at Azalea Avenue. "Watch where you're going," hollers Mr. Wallingham.

I signal my thanks for his not smushing me and speed ahead to I don't know where. I just keep running.

Mr. Wallingham didn't go to the war because he has bad eyesight. If my daddy had poor eyes, none of this silliness with Mama would be happening. Daddy would have been here all along. How can Mama marry someone else? How can she do this to me? How can she do this to Daddy?

I look both ways and dash across the street. Ruby Jane and Delilah walk out of the library just as I jump onto the sidewalk. They each hold books in their arms. Homer walks between them with a plastic sword attached to his belt and his ever-present railroad cap on his head.

"Everything okay?" Ruby Jane asks as I fly by. "Wanna get a float with us?"

I don't have time to answer.

I have to go somewhere to think. Someplace where no one will bother me. Or find me for a while, if they come looking. In the distance, the flag on top of the Gladiola train station waves. An empty bench at the station is the perfect place to think. I run faster, gulping in the chilly air.

The sky turns darker and darker as black clouds swoop in. It's just after four o'clock, but it looks like eight o'clock at night. Cars turn on their headlights. I reach the corner of State and Main in no time, dart down the steps, cross the intersection, and run back up onto the sidewalk on the other side. Folks peer out the window of the pharmacy and point upward.

Ping, ping, ping.

Tiny hailstones fall, like rice on a tin roof. I throw my arms over my head. The prickles don't stop. Shoppers scramble inside buildings as I run through bouncing pellets.

Bam, bam, bam, bam. The hail comes big, hard, and fast.

"Get inside," calls Mr. Wyatt from the *Gladiola Gazette*.

No, I can't stop. I can't stop running. Running to the tracks.

Four blasts of a train whistle sound. A train is approaching. Just ahead its engine noses into the station. The northbound 4:01 is late.

I stop cold.

It's a sign.

By tomorrow morning a connection on the westbound Texas Eagle will roll into Fort Worth, the drop-off point for the Texas Merci boxcar. Why should I sit on a bench and stew, when I can catch a train and meet my daddy? I'll bring him home. And that will stop Mama's foolishness once and for all.

Bam, bam, bam.

Cars pull over, and their occupants cover their ears to block out the noise. It sounds like garbage can lids banging together.

Bam. Bam. Bam.

The hail beats down on my head. Beats my arms and shoulders, even through my coat. My heart booms as loud as the hail. The street and sidewalk turn white.

I take off again.

My destination is half a block and a hail-covered picnic area away. If I hurry, I can catch that train.

Running on hail is like running on marbles, and I have to slow. I tiptoe-hop my way across the slippery sidewalk.

Bam. Bam. Bam. CRACK.

My feet go out from under me, and I land hard on the cold, bumpy concrete. Pain shoots up my spine and into my head. A line zigzags across the front window of a car next to the curb, from one side to the other.

I take an extra-deep breath and wiggle my toes and fingers like Ruby Jane learned in first aid. I am still in one piece.

Ping, ping, ping.

The storm wanes.

I scramble up and keep going.

thirty

THE WORD "stowaway" was invented for people like me.

There are advantages to being the granddaughter of a rail-road man. I've heard stories of all the different places folks have hidden when they didn't purchase a ticket. It's time to put this knowledge to use. No purse. No cash. No problem.

"Last call for Texas Eagle Twenty-Two," Mr. Samuels, the train master, calls as I peek from behind the bench at the station. "All aboard."

He takes out his pocket watch, strides a ways down the platform, pivots, and heads in the other direction. Steam billows like clouds beneath the wheels and then disappears as it rises. Most of the windows in the gleaming blue-and-silver passenger cars are closed. A woman and young boy stand on the platform beside one lowered halfway. The woman holds the hand of a man on board.

All's clear. I spring from my hiding place behind the bench and hope I won't slip on the hail.

Someone calls my name.

I know that voice. I keep going. "What are you doing here?" Ben asks, sliding to meet me halfway across the wooden platform.

"Leaving," I say, and move closer to the train. "It's too crowded around here right now."

"Where you headed?"

"Fort Worth," I whisper before I can stop myself, and step backward toward the train car.

"Me too," he whispers back.

I look at him hard. "Have you been planning this trip for a while? 'Cause I haven't heard you talk about it."

"It was a last-minute decision," he says, and puts his hands in his coat pockets. "You?"

I don't believe him for a second. He was on his way into my house when I last saw him. I scrunch my eyebrows together and try to read his mind. "You don't need to come with me."

I turn and dash up the steps between two passenger cars.

"Roger that," says Ben, and follows. "It's my choice."

Two long blasts scream across the station, and the train jerks forward. As far as I can tell, we are in the middle of the train. We stand on the top step, clutch the hand railings, and hold on.

I am on my way! And apparently, so is Ben.

Daddy always said there is nothing better than a surprise. This will be the best one ever.

The train station disappears as we trundle around a bend and pick up speed. The ground, thick with ice crystals, sparkles in the now bright sun and makes the world seem less cold.

That cold, like downing a Dr Pepper float at the soda fountain too fast, has given me a brain freeze.

"You don't happen to have any extra money on you, do you?" I ask him.

Ben turns his pockets inside out and shrugs. Last minute, indeed.

"Ben Truman, are you following me? Because I don't need a bodyguard."

"Affirmative. I think you need a friend."

"Oh. Well, friend, just don't get caught."

I crouch next to the door of the passenger car that faces north and, in slow motion, lift my head and peep in the window. No one looks back. Row after row, folks sit facing back and front. Ladies wear their Sunday best with matching hats, and the men in suits and hats too. Not a seat is empty. I rub the arms of my coat. Everyone inside looks toasty and warm.

One man reads a newspaper, and a lady wearing a peacock-blue hat plays cards with a child in a red cap. The man leaning his head against a window is probably asleep. Everyone else is staring out the windows at the blanket of hail that stretches farther than far.

The forward door of the train car flies open, and the

conductor, in his black uniform and hat, strolls in, ready to collect from the folks who've just boarded. In moments, he'll move on to the next car.

It is time for hide-and-seek. Only, I have no intention of being found.

I push open the door to the car behind us. Ben follows. Folks glance up from their food and conversations, and I nod. This is the lounge car—half–private dining, half-sleeping. *Pretend you belong here*, I tell myself. I march down the center aisle, sure-footed so as not to end up in someone's lap. The train rocks ever so slightly as I pass men and women seated in comfy blue chairs, enjoying beverages and snacks. Later, they will retreat to their private compartments to rest. People pay big money to sleep lying down.

At the bar, the aisle takes a jog to the left. I make a beeline toward the shower at the end of the car—a perfect place to hide. The train picks up speed. I bump against compartment door C, right myself, and keep going. Just before I reach the end of the car and the shower in the bathroom, nature calls.

I scoot in and lock the door behind me.

When I am done, I lean my ear against the door. No footsteps. No voices. I swing open the door. *Clunk.*

"Ouch!"

"I'm sor—" I say as I poke my head around the door.

Ben stands in the aisle as an older woman speeds toward us down the narrow space behind him, signaling her need for the facility. I step out and stand next to the windows.

Ben stretches his arms across the aisle to hold steady.

Over his shoulder, the conductor is only footsteps away.

There's nowhere else to hide.

I fling open the door of the sleeper compartment beside me and scramble in. I put my finger to my lips and pray the lady with curlers poking out of her nightcap won't say a word. She must be napping before supper. The woman scrunches herself against the corner of her bed, grabs her blanket to her chin, and screams. The man on the top bunk stirs. "Get out. Out!" he hollers.

The door whips open and the conductor grabs me by the arm. "Come with me, young lady. Now."

Ben and I are thrown off the train at the next station.

If only I hadn't run into him. Now I'll never make it to Fort Worth. Daddy will have to travel down here by himself.

The train was a sign. A sign of failure.

thirty-one

MR. HUCKLEBERRY, the stationmaster, puts down the phone in his office. "The granddaughter of William Bennett? Of all people, you should know better than to pull a shenanigan like this."

Ben and I sit in comfy chairs beside a potbellied stove, with blankets around our shoulders and cups of hot cocoa in our hands. The room is toasty except for the occasional sharp blast of cold air when someone opens the door. Which so far has happened three times.

I told Mr. Huckleberry right off that I was sorry, though I didn't mean it, and that I'd pay the railroad back for the ticket.

"They're sending someone to pick up the two of you," he says, rising from his chair. He opens the door. "Your grandpa said to stay put," he adds, and walks out.

"What'll happen when you get home?" asks Ben.

"I'll be grounded for the rest of my life. You?"

"Probably sore for a week."

"You shouldn't have followed me."

"I wasn't about to bail out on you." Ben's voice is serious yet his eyes twinkle. "Are you okay?"

"Yes." *No. People think my mama may be getting married again. And not to my daddy. My Wall of Fame is still empty. Other than that, I'm hunky-dory.*

"Good. I mean, I'm sure everyone that saw you running to the train was worried." He takes a sip of cocoa. "What's in Fort Worth?"

"The drop-off point of the Merci boxcar. I thought it would be swell to meet it."

"You know it's not coming until next week, right?"

"I believe in being early. Besides, I was planning to stay with my aunt in Dallas." *Which actually would have been a great idea. It's close to Fort Worth.*

It's time to stop his inquisition. "Ever been to the budding metropolis of Tula before?" I elbow Ben. *Tula is smaller than Gladiola.*

"Negative," he says, putting down his cup.

"Let's have a look around," I say, and grab a piece of paper and a pencil:

Dear Mr. Huckleberry,
   We want to explore the station. Be back soon.

Your new pals,
Glory Bea and Ben

Ben opens the door and walks out into the sunshine. The ground is still white with ice crystals. It is beautiful.

"Quick," he says, picking up a handful of hail at the end of the platform.

I back against the building. "Don't you dare."

Ben laughs. "No, I was going to say that we should build a hailman before it all melts."

The streets have started to thaw, so if we put together Mr. Hail in the shade, he just might last a few hours or more.

"Let's," I say.

So next to the building, Ben and I make the first bona fide hailman the Tula train station has probably ever seen. Ben gives the hailman his hat.

I squat, put my arm around our icy figure, and smile as Ben snaps his imaginary camera. I'm not cold anymore. "Wait, this is Tula, Texas!" I shout.

"Affirmative. Doubt it's changed since you said that minutes ago."

"There's someone here I need to see." And I take off toward the stationmaster's office. Surely he knows everyone in town.

"Who?" calls Ben, catching up.

"Mr. Lloyd Huffman."

"Because . . ."

"Because," I say as my hand clamps around the office door handle, "I read about him in the newspaper."

He is the miracle man.

thirty-two

OF COURSE Mr. Huckleberry knows everyone in Tula. And demands we return in thirty minutes. So here we are, standing in front of Mr. Lloyd Huffman's property. The blinds on every window of the tiny wood frame house are drawn, although light shines around their edges. Smoke curls up from the chimney. A cedar fire, no doubt, from the sweet, woody smell. Someone is home.

"You going to stand out here in the cold or knock on their door?" asks Ben.

What am I waiting for?

A girl about my age wearing braids down to her waist answers the door and lets us in. A family of three sits around a square card table eating supper. The house smells like chicken and dumplings.

"Well, hello, strangers," says the mother, waving her napkin.

"Mr. Huckleberry called to say we could expect you."

The mother, in cat-eye glasses, sits across from a teenage boy in a long-sleeved plaid shirt. Steam drifts up from three bowls on the table.

Ben and I move closer. "Hello to you too. I'm Glory Bea Bennett from Gladiola, and this is my friend Ben Truman.

"I was hoping to talk to Mr. Lloyd Huffman, ma'am," I say as I stand beside the table. My voice has raised an octave and I clear my throat. "I read about his amnesia in the *Gladiola Gazette* and wanted to ask him some questions."

"You just missed him," says the girl. She plops back into her chair. "He took the train to New York yesterday. You're not going to believe it. They want him to be on a TV show, and a bunch of important doctors want to study his brain."

I examine the multicolored braided rug under my feet.

"A day late and a dollar short," says Ben.

That is no joke.

"Don't worry," says the girl. She smiles. "This time Daddy will be back in just a few weeks. Pleeeeease come for another visit. Daddy likes to tell his story."

"Thank you," I say. "That's a very kind offer." I don't know if I can take her up on it. No telling how long I'll be grounded for today's escapades, and by then the boxcar will have come and gone.

My stomach gurgles and I put my hand over my tummy. I mumble, "Sorry." Except for the hot cocoa at the station, I haven't eaten anything since a skimpy PB&J at lunch.

"Dear me, I've forgotten my manners," says Mrs. Huffman, getting up. "Why, as you're from Gladiola, we're practically neighbors. Please join us for dinner, won't you?"

"Thank you," I say, "but we can't."

"Why not?" asks Ben, eyeing the tasty meal.

I motion toward the wall clock. We used up half our time traipsing over here.

"I'm sure you know Miss Connie Partridge," said Mrs. Huffman, moving toward the kitchen.

"Everyone in Gladiola talks to her," I say. "She's the switchboard operator."

"I knew we had a connection," says Mrs. Huffman. "Connie and I go back to our high school days in Wichita Falls. Mercy, I haven't seen her in a month of Sundays."

Mrs. Huffman looks to her children. "Clayton and Meredith, make room at the table."

"Thank you kindly," I say. "Really"—I pull on the sleeve of Ben's jacket—"we've got to go." Even though I have oodles of questions like: What took him so long? Did he look the same? Did he remember everything about his life from before he left? I say, "Our ride is probably waiting for us right now."

"I understand," says Mrs. Huffman.

"Before we run off," I say, folding my hands together, "I'd like to know . . . when Mr. Huffman came back, did he . . . did he remember all of you?"

The family exchanges glances.

"Everyone except me," says Meredith.

I take in a sharp breath.

"I was a surprise," she says, and lifts her arms into the air. "Mama didn't know she was pregnant when he left."

I blow out a long breath. "Thank you, thank you so much for your hospitality."

"I'm sorry we can't stay," says Ben. He glares at me. "Real sorry."

"We hope to see you again," I say.

"We'd like nothing better," says Mrs. Huffman. "Give our best to Connie."

"Yes, ma'am," I say.

We turn to the door, and most of all I wonder, did the Huffmans ever give up hope?

As we trudge back to the station, Ben says, "You know my dad came back different, Glory Bea." He kicks a mound of slushy, muddy hail. "I lost him to the war," he says, and slows to a stop.

I stop too. Ben's never said that before.

"He's here, but he's not here, you know?"

"I do know. I'm sorry, Ben."

My friend's eyes close. Then he looks right at me. "Do you ever think about what would have happened if your dad had come home?"

I meet his gaze.

"All the time," I say.

"If he'd returned like mine?"

I shake my head at the ground. Daddy like Mr. Truman? That's never occurred to me. I don't want to think about it.

"I wonder what's worse, Glory Bea. A broken dad . . . or one who is never coming back."

I flinch.

Ben's eyes soften. "I know you miss your dad too. I remember him. He was always smiling."

If there's one thing I know, it's this—when my daddy returns, he will help Ben make up some of the difference. I hope. I pray.

thirty-three

WE RUSH BY Grandpa's car parked in front of the station. No one is inside. I sure hope Mama isn't with him.

"Ready for the court-martial?" asks Ben.

"I'll tell them it was all my fault—which it was. That should help you."

Ben shakes his head.

"And if you don't mind," I say, "please don't say anything about Fort Worth."

"Deal," he says, and holds out his hand.

We make it official and spit-shake on it.

Ben and I hop onto the platform and head straight for the stationmaster's office. They must have heard us coming, because the door swings open. Out walk Mr. Huckleberry and Randall Horton.

I skid to a stop.

"I volunteered," Randall Horton says to the question we don't ask.

"Who else is with you?"

"I traveled solo."

Ben scratches his head. "Why you?"

"I've never been to Tula before," Randall Horton says. "Glory Bea's grandpa offered his car, and I thought it would be nice to take a little drive." He turns to Mr. Huckleberry and shakes his hand. "Nice to meet you, sir. Thanks for taking care of the runaways."

For the record, I wasn't running away. I was running *to*.

"Glad to help," says Mr. Huckleberry.

Ben and I thank Mr. Huckleberry for his hospitality. He might have been sore at us, but at least he didn't yell.

"Tula's pretty small," I say to Randall Horton as we walk away. "There's not much to see. Especially when it turns dark."

"I wouldn't mind coming back, day or night," says Randall Horton. "The people are nice, and your grandpa says throngs come from miles around to eat the fried catfish and hush puppies at their roadside café."

"We could stop on the way out of town, sir," suggests Ben.

"I wish we could," says Randall Horton. "I promised your families I'd have you back stat."

"Darn," says Ben.

"That's why I picked up an order to go," says Randall Horton.

"Hooyah!" says Ben.

"I'm not hungry," I say.

"I thought—" Ben starts, and I jab him in the side.

Ben rubs his hands together. "Glory Bea, I'd be happy to eat your share."

As if on cue, my stomach grumbles.

"Interesting," says Ben, looking up to the sky and shaking his head. "Thunder on a clear evening."

Randall Horton keeps walking. Maybe he didn't hear. He unlocks the back car door and holds it open for us. "I ran away once when I was about your age."

"Where to?" Ben asks as we climb inside.

Two small white to-go boxes, a bottle of Coca-Cola, and another of Dr Pepper lean against the seat. Ben takes in an exaggerated breath through his nose. Crispy fried catfish, crunchy and sweet hush puppies.

I don't want it to, but my mouth waters. Ben digs right in.

Randall Horton hurries around to the front, slides in, and starts the car. "I headed for my grandmother's apartment across a bridge to Manhattan." He looks at us in the rearview mirror. "You kids made it farther than I did. I only got to the end of the block."

With that, he turns on the radio and pulls out of the station. Bing Crosby sings "I'll Be Seeing You," and Randall Horton joins him.

I fold my arms across my chest and lean back into the seat.

My mistake, not thinking of going to Fort Worth earlier. If I had, I could have made a plan. A successful one.

Ben deposits another hush puppy into his mouth and scoots forward. He hangs his arms over the front seat. "How much trouble are we in, Mr. Horton?"

"Everyone was more worried than angry."

Ben taps the front seat cushion in time with the music and slides back to his seat. My stomach is aching, but I refuse to accept this gift from that man.

Between bites of his own food, Randall Horton sings the words to every song the whole way home.

How annoying.

thirty-four

MAMA IS THE ONLY one around when I get home. She must have asked Grams and Grandpa for privacy. She hugs me so hard, it hurts. Randall Horton doesn't come in.

I draw tiny circles with my finger on the table in the foyer while Mama waves good night to him. Then I wait for her to tell me that I'll have to do dishes for the rest of my life, be grounded until next year, or be banned from painting in Grandpa's studio for who knows how long.

Mama says, "I hope you thanked Randall."

I forgot.

Mama says, "We need to talk."

No, we don't.

Mama says, "I want you to be happy."

I will when Randall Horton goes away.

Mama says, "Stubbornness is a very unattractive quality, Glory Bea."

I stomp upstairs.

She follows.

Mama does not understand. In nine days she will. She'll forgive me for everything then—the pie disaster, tossing Randall Horton's letters, the time I didn't relay his tardiness, running off today. She'll thank me for protecting her from making the biggest mistake of her life.

Mama perches beside me on the edge of my bed and takes my hands in hers. Her eyes show disappointment. "Glory Bea Bennett, you put yourself in great danger." Her clasp tightens and her eyes fire up. "Who knows what *could* have happened. I've already lost your father."

No, Mama. You haven't. We haven't. You'll see.

I wriggle my hands free.

"Your actions hurt people. Today's escapade . . ."

I pick at one of the soft tufts on my chenille bedspread. When I was little, I used to pretend they were puffs of dandelions and that I slept in a bed filled with wishes. Tonight, they're a field of measles. Itchy, irritated bumps.

"I'm sorry, Mama, but . . ."

"No buts. Running away never solves a problem. I know you didn't intend to hurt us. That is not who you are. Nevertheless . . ."

Mama trembles.

I have hurt people who have been kind to me.

"I'm sorry, Mama."

"You've been acting out, Glory Bea. That's not like you. Ignoring it hasn't seemed to help. Nor hinting. Nor kindness. You've been sabotaging my relationship with Randall. I don't appreciate it."

Wait. Now we're talking about Randall Horton?

"At the very least, I expect you to be civil to him. He is a very good friend of this family."

"How good?"

"We are talking about your behavior."

Mama gives me an extra-hard squeeze. "I love you, Glory Bea." And she retreats to her room.

I should talk to Grams and Grandpa. They'll help me talk some sense into Mama.

A light shines under their bedroom door.

I kneel down and put my ear to the opening.

"He's going to ask her any day now," says Grandpa.

"I'm glad you gave our blessing," says Grams.

No. No. NO times infinity!

Their doorknob turns and I dash into my room. Shaking.

I may have spoken out loud.

thirty-five

I WAKE UP hungry. So hungry.

And last night I was tired. So very tired. Most likely I mis-understood what Grandpa and Grams said. After all, I didn't hear the before and after. Maybe Randall Horton wants to take Mama to the Valentine's Dance. Or on a trip. Or maybe they were talking about another he and another she. It's Grams's business, after all.

I will not panic. I have a plan. There's no need to change it.

"Eggs and sausage and toast for breakfast," says Grams, handing me a plate of food as I rush into the kitchen.

"Merci."

Mama and Grandpa are already at the table eating.

"Storm that big means it's time to clean up around here," says Grams, bringing the coffeepot to the table.

I blink. No more questions about my trip? No talk about consequences? No mention of what I said last night? I take a seat at the table. That is a-okay by me.

"After Randall gets off work today, he and Grandpa will help the McGraths cut up their tree limbs," says Grams. "Then they will tackle our yard."

Mama and I raise our eyebrows. We know what she will say next.

"Spring cleaning inside and out?" I ask. "In February?"

"Yes," says Grams. "Glory Bea, I know you have outgrown some of your clothes. I want you to go through your closet and dresser after school. We'll place the things you can no longer wear in a new home. The glee club is in charge of a clothing booth at the Veterans' Fund-Raiser in a few months, and I'm sure you can make a donation."

"I think I might clean out George's closet," says Mama.

She doesn't appear to be kidding.

Like the rest of the house, everything in their room is just as it was the day Daddy left—the pictures on their dresser, his handkerchiefs in the top right-hand drawer, the two drawers of underwear and socks underneath. In the closet, to the right of Mama's clothes, are his trousers and shirts and jackets and ties. On the floor beneath, his shoes are lined up just so. Newly polished.

Nothing has changed.

Nothing.

He can step right back in.

Grams puts her hand on top of Mama's.

"Only if you are ready," she says.

Mama nods. "I think it's time, Melba."

"No, it's not," I say.

I ball my hands and press them together.

"You can't throw out all of Daddy's things."

"There are men in need of good clothing, Glory Bea. Your daddy's clothes aren't doing anyone any good hanging in a closet."

"Don't," I say. "Please. Not yet."

"Today is the day, Glory Bea."

My insides are as scrambled as the eggs on my plate.

"We should keep everything," I say.

They are moving on.

Someone else will fill up the spaces.

"I don't want to see other men wearing his clothes." My voice cracks and I can feel my eyes filling. "At least put them in the attic."

"We'll see."

The phone rings and I run to catch it. Ruby Jane asks me to meet her at the corner so we can walk to school together. "Five minutes," I say, and hang up.

I head upstairs for my books, raid my piggy bank, and hop

back into the kitchen. "Ruby Jane said she'd go with me to pay for my ticket to Tula before school."

"See you later," says Mama.

She forgets to call me "sugar."

I grab a piece of toast to settle my stomach, and leave.

thirty-six

"YOU AND BEN are the talk of the town," says Ruby Jane as soon as I walk up. "Riding on the train by yourselves? I can only imagine. Nothing that exciting ever happens to me."

I try to smile, only all I can think about is the biggest mistake in the world my mama is about to make. I tighten my coat belt. It's still cold. You'd never know it hailed yesterday—the streets are dry.

"Don't leave out a single detail," says Ruby Jane.

I don't tell her why I went. I don't tell her about the Huffmans. I can't bear to see an inkling of doubt on her face. Not now. Not when the boxcar is almost here. Not when Randall Horton won't leave. Not when Mama is throwing everything away. As Grandpa would say, it's "full steam ahead." I must keep the faith. So I tell her about the train, the hailman, the cocoa, and the ride home.

"Glory Bea, did Ben talk about me? Ask about me?"

I rub my nose. "We jabbered about so many different things, I can't remember."

I am a dreadful matchmaker. It never occurred to me to talk up Ruby Jane or pump Ben for more info. The trip was about Daddy.

"All that time with Ben," she says. "I wish it'd been me."

"Tell you what, as soon as we get to school, let's track him down and you can ask him a question."

Ruby Jane nibbles on her mitten. "Okay."

We search for Ben in all his usual hangouts—locker, homeroom, front hallway, and library. We ask five different people if they've seen him, and get the same answer—no.

"Maybe he slept in," says Ruby Jane.

"More likely grounded," I say. Because of me. "If he shows, we'll catch him at lunch. Be positive."

"I'll try."

"There's Delilah and Harry. Let's pull her away for a sec and fill her in."

"He's here!" Ruby Jane squeals as we scan the cafeteria at lunch.

Ben walks straight toward us, all smiles.

Ruby Jane stiffens beside me.

"Smile," says Delilah. "Wave."

Ruby Jane moves in a rigid jerky Frankenstein way.

When Ben is within earshot, she blurts, "IF YOU COULD

HAVE LUNCH WITH ANYONE IN THE WORLD, WHO WOULD IT BE?"

The kids at the tables around us gawk, but Ruby Jane doesn't notice. Her eyes are on Ben.

"Outstanding question, Ruby Jane," he says. "Let me think about that."

Then he raises his eyebrows at me. "You okay?"

"Yes. You?"

"Affirmative."

"To get back to your question, Ruby Jane," says Ben, "I would like to have lunch with you and Delilah and Glory Bea."

Her face colors ruby red.

"Follow us," says Delilah, and points the way with her baton.

Ruby Jane asks two more questions. Only, this time they're for all of us. Who knew both Delilah and Ben would choose to eat pickles? Or that one Christmas Eve, Delilah set her parents' nightstand clock forward two hours, while Ben's best trick was the purse stunt he played on me.

When the bell rings, Ruby Jane floats back to our classroom. "See, I've been practicing," she says.

I take a detour after school. Bradley's Bait & Tackle is pinch-my-nose worthy. "A small container of night crawlers, please," I say, and place money on the crowded counter between a high-priced tackle box and the cash register.

"Coming right up," says Mr. Bradley. His plaid shirt has

patches on the elbows but his denim overalls look brand-new. "Going fishing with your grandpa?"

Nope, with my daddy. Of course I don't say that. I pay and leave.

To my surprise, Ben is outside. "Really," he says, "how did it go last night?"

"A lecture. No consequences."

Ben digs his hands into his pockets and we start home.

"What about you?" I ask.

"Randall Horton walked me inside, sat down with my parents, and told them about our drive back, including his story about running away."

"And?"

"They laughed."

"Laughed?"

"Randall Horton is a good guy, Glory Bea. You know he came over the day Dad returned from the hospital. He's been by every day since. They play chess together. It helps my dad take his mind off darker things."

I didn't have a clue.

"Everyone in our town is polite to my dad, but his old friends have dropped away. They don't invite him and Mama out anymore." Ben winces, like he's plunged his hands into freezing water. "Your grandpa hasn't stopped asking. My dad never accepts. You know it's hard for my dad to socialize."

Ben shakes his head before he continues. "Seven years is a

long time, Glory Bea. Randall Horton understands what my dad went through. Not that others don't; it's just that they aren't interested in the war anymore. It helps my dad to talk. Soldier to soldier. Randall Horton hasn't heard my daddy's stories. It means a lot to have someone listen to him. He's the best thing that's happened to my dad in a long time."

"I'm happy your dad has a friend, Ben."

My daddy might too.

thirty-seven

MAMA IS ALREADY home. I know because her bedroom door is closed. From my room two doors down, I hear her phonograph playing "The Glory of Love." It is the song she and Daddy courted to.

I flop onto my bed and glare at my ceiling. The tiny round tufts on my bedspread make pinkish indents on my arm.

My daddy needs his clothes. He can't wear his uniform all the time. He'll want to put on one of his favorite shirts. I like the blue-and-white Hawaiian print the best. Ben's daddy sent it to him when he was stationed at Pearl Harbor, in thanks for checking on his family. Then the bombs fell. And Daddy signed up.

The song "My Happiness" plays next. It's Mama's new favorite and she joins in. She's not a great singer, although she has lots of enthusiasm.

Tap-tap. Ta-tap-tap. Tap-tap.

It's Grams's special knock.

"Come in."

"Would you like some assistance, Glory Bea?" she asks, holding an empty cardboard box.

"I don't think so, thanks."

"Holler if you change your mind."

"Grams," I say, sitting up. "Isn't there something we can do to stop this? I'm his daughter. You're his mother."

Grams smiles gently. "It's your mama's journey too."

She sets down the box next to my desk that spills over with valentines makings for my classmates and family. "They're volunteering to chaperone with us at the Valentine's Day Dance next week," she says quietly, and tiptoes out.

So Grams and Grandpa's conversation was about Randall Horton wanting Mama's help with the dance. *Fine. Go. Go to the dance, Mama. It won't matter. Daddy's coming two days later.*

The wind outside is gusty. The tops of the trees sway like someone is standing on the ground, shaking their trunks. A bare branch snaps on the pecan outside my window—it is V-shaped and snagged by a lower branch.

I glance at my closet door. I will start cleaning when that branch falls.

A big gust of wind rattles my windows, and I move to the sill. The thin branch sails away.

"There she blows," hollers Grandpa from below.

Grandpa and Randall Horton have moved their cleanup campaign to the front yard.

Just like that, a bonus New Year's resolution effort flies into my head and I zip downstairs and out the door.

Randall Horton is picking up branches near the street, while Grandpa is closer to the house.

I reach for a twig near Randall Horton and snap it in two. "I heard about you and Mama and the dance."

"Glad to help," he says, straightening up. "I'll miss the start but will come as soon as I finish up at the pharmacy."

"Well, seeing as you're new to Gladiola and all, I thought you should know there's an important tradition all the grown-up men follow."

I spot a weed in the grass next to my shoes and yank it out. "I'm all ears."

"Everyone comes in costume. I'm told one time Grandpa came as a pirate, but his all-time best was when he showed up as an armadillo."

Grandpa could have. Would have. If given the chance.

"Wish I could have been there to see that, Glory Bea. I'm definitely going to have to think about this. Thanks for giving me the inside scoop."

"You're welcome," I say, and throw the weed onto the pile of debris. "Oh, I almost forgot. It's always a surprise."

Randall Horton gives me a thumbs-up.

That ought to keep him busy. The less time with Mama the better.

"By the way, I need to learn how to play chess ASAP. Can you teach me?"

I can't believe I'm asking. But as Grams says: "Desperate times call for desperate measures."

"I'd be honored, Glory Bea. We can start after I finish here."

"Thank you, thank you," I say, and zoom back inside.

Grams is on the phone so I slow as I climb the stairs.

"I love your plans," she says. "A scavenger hunt that ends atop the water tower is a fitting introduction to your town. I'll let you know if she's afraid of heights."

She ends the call and begins another. "Connie, I've got a quick question for you."

Someone is about to have a big adventure.

Upstairs, I begin grabbing clothes off the hangers and toss them onto my bed. I pick my shoes off the closet floor and add them to the pile. I move back and forth until my bed is a mound of dresses, skirts, blouses, and shoes to be excavated. I reach deep into the dark for the last few things, and my big toe slams into something hard. I hop back on one foot and crumble to the floor, rocking back and forth to ease the pain.

My jack-in-the-box. It was a birthday gift from Daddy. I pick it up and hold it tight. I think about how I would sit on Daddy's lap, buried in his arms, and wind it up. Every time the clown popped up, I'd scream, half-scared, half-excited.

Daddy was always there with a hug and a laugh.

"Don't be afraid, sweet pea," he'd say, and I'd wind it up again.

An hour later, there's a knock on my door. "Randall can give you a quick lesson before dinner," Grandpa says.

I join him in the study downstairs.

"Pretend like I've never played before," I tell Randall Horton. Because it's true.

"Each piece has a different role and moves in a different way," he says, and he shows me what they can do.

We clear the board and I practice moving the white pieces.

"Most times, the game is won by checkmate."

There's a monumental amount to learn, and my head is already full. "Thanks for the lesson," I say. "I need to go and help with dinner."

"You're a quick learner, Glory Bea. Let me know when you're ready for round two. Your daddy would be proud of you, you know."

"Thanks." I don't correct him, but he should have used the present tense. *Is proud.*

The Most Important French Words and Phrases (According to *Moi*)

1. *Je t'aime* (Zhuh tem) I love you

2. *Oh là là* (O la la) Oh boy!

3. *Je suis si heureux de vous revoir!* (Zhuh swee see ehruh da vu rev wah) I am so happy to see you again!

4. *Tu me manques tellement* (Too meh manck telemon) I miss you so much

5. *Bon retour de la France* (Bohn reh tour da la France) Welcome home/back from France

Did You Know?

Gladiola Gazette

February 9, 1948

Are your hearts all aflutter, Gladies?

Tickets for the annual Valentine's Day Dance at Gladiola Primary and Intermediate are almost sold out. Proceeds will benefit the school library. Don't delay! Something unforgettable always transpires.

Remember who won the "Name That Love Song" contest last year?*

Daisy Smithers's answer to Grant Jordan's proposal in 1940?*

The champions of our longest-ever jitterbug marathon in 1944?*

What, oh what, will ensue this year?

No interest in cutting a rug? There's still a place on the dance floor for you. To chaperone, call Mrs. Jerald Andersen, #27, today.

Finally, as a public service, devoted readers, I'd like to remind you (in French, the language of love) of the most perfect and popular gift ideas for your amour:

bouquet des fleurs (bouquet of flowers),
des bonbons (candy), *du parfum* (perfume),
des bijoux (jewelry).

So now you know, dear Gladies, now you
know,

Penny Pfluger

*Conner McGrath (age 10, visiting from
Houston), grandson of Mr. and Mrs. Steven
McGrath; Daisy declined (she and Grant
were 7 years old); Coach Allen and Miss
Betty X. Johnson (both over 21).

thirty-eight

ON THE EVE of Valentine's Day, I sit at my desk adding an extra helping of silver glitter to a paper heart that says *Be Mine* when Mama calls me for supper. Other valentines that I've spent the last two afternoons decorating cover my floor and dresser and desk. Valentines that I signed in red pencil with my name and title—*Glory Bea Bennett, Matchmaker Extraordinaire.*

I am in serious need of success.

Sometimes you have to take decisive action. I slide down the banister, land on my feet, and run to the phone.

"Miss Connie, please connect me to number twenty-nine."

"You mean your next-door neighbors, *oui?*"

"Oui."

"Mademoiselle Bennett, can't you just walk over there instead of tying up the line?"

I don't answer.

Ring. Ring.

"Truman here."

"Mr. Truman, may I please speak to Ben?"

"Glory Bea, is that you? Why don't you just come over?"

I twist the phone cord around my free hand.

"Ben. Telephone."

"Hello."

"Would you like to take Ruby Jane Pfluger to the Valentine's Day Dance?"

"No."

"Are you sure? She's really nice and I think she likes you."

"No."

"Is that a yes no, a maybe no, or a no no?"

"Double no."

"Okay, bye."

That didn't go so well.

"Uh, Glory Bea," says Ben.

"Yes."

"You can tell Ruby Jane to save a dance for me."

"I will."

I put the receiver to my heart and hold it tight.

"*Allô?*" says Miss Connie. "*Allô?* Glory Bea. Either hang up or ask me to make another call."

Ruby Jane answers on the first ring.

"Ben requested that you save a dance for him tomorrow night."

I pull the receiver away from my ear and cover it with my palm as fast as I can.

When my friend takes a breath from screaming, I jump back in. "You won't be going to the dance with him like you'd hoped. No double date."

"This is a start, right?" says Ruby Jane.

"Right."

"Good, because I made a valentine for him that I'll slip into his locker before school. I signed it 'From Your Secret Admirer.' What do you think?" she asks me.

"Why not?"

"Exactly," says Ruby Jane.

thirty-nine

RUBY JANE got one more valentine than everyone else in our class today. Only, not from Ben. Our classmate Toby Mickelson sent it via his mama from his hospital bed, where he is in traction for a broken leg. "I guess it's because I dropped by after my first-aid class on Saturday and played checkers," Ruby Jane says.

"I guess," I answer.

The Valentine's Day Dance begins at six thirty. Ruby Jane and I are ready at four. I wear my pink poodle skirt, white blouse, and pink sweater. She wears her red party dress. Her hair is pulled off her face with two white barrettes. Soft curls fall to her shoulders. Her perm has relaxed. This is the look we were after two weeks ago.

Ruby Jane's coat lies across the back of my desk chair. She

reaches into the pocket, pulls something out, and slips it behind her back. "Guess."

"Right," I say.

Ruby Jane brings her hands in front of her and opens up her right hand.

"Lipstick? You get to wear lipstick?"

"Not just me. Us. It's called First Dance."

"It's perfect," we both say at the same time.

"Just don't tell my mama," I say.

"Never," says Ruby Jane, and puts a line of blushing pink on the top of my hand between my thumb and forefinger to check the color. "It was made for you," she says.

"Look at this wall," I say, pointing to the one behind my dresser. "Imagine a photo of you and Ben."

Ruby Jane's eyes crinkle. "If that happens—"

"No, *when* that happens," I interrupt.

Ruby Jane twirls. "It would be the best thing ever."

Almost.

Since we want to be wrinkle free, we stand beside the kitchen counter and eat Grams's deluxe homemade burgers. For extra insurance, we cover up with aprons so we won't drip mustard and ketchup onto our clothes.

"Grams," I ask, "may I put in a request for meat loaf, mashed potatoes, green beans, and pecan pie for supper on the sixteenth?" It's Daddy's favorite.

"You surely may," she says.

"*Très bien, merci!*" I say, and kiss her on each cheek.

After supper, Grandpa volunteers for kitchen duty, and Grams hightails it to my school to help set up. Ruby Jane and I move to the parlor and stand by the blue wing chairs while I quiz her on current events.

When Grandpa walks in with his gold watch in his hand and announces it is six fifteen, we put on our coats. There is a most enormous bouquet of red carnations on the front table. Grandpa must have used up all his savings. I lean in to take in the smells. That's when I see the card with print like an architect's.

I shake off the name. Randall Horton can send all the flowers he wants. My daddy is coming back the day after tomorrow, and Randall Horton will be known as a friend of the family.

Red and white streamers and balloons hang from the ceiling of the school cafeteria turned dance hall, along with paper hearts. Chairs ring the room. Folks cluster in groups holding punch cups or are on the dance floor.

The band onstage wears top hats. Our school principal plays fiddle, and Mr. McGrath the guitar. They start "I'm Looking Over a Four-Leaf Clover."

I clutch my bracelet. Ruby Jane holds her arms tight across her body and twists in time to the music. Her curls move from side to side just so.

"I am so nervous, I can hardly stand it," she says.

Delilah and Harry Ackerman swing and sway to the music. Minus her baton.

"Look, there's Ben, on the far side of the floor with Claire," I say.

Ruby Jane springs in place.

Ben whirls Claire around. They make their way over to us when the song ends.

"Fruit punch, everyone?" Ben asks.

"In a minute," says Claire. "I'm going to the powder room."

"YES, PLEASE," says Ruby Jane, and looks him in the eye.

She sounds good. Confident, even. The shouting? It doesn't matter. It's already noisy in here.

"There's someone I need to catch," I say. "See you later." Ruby Jane is ready. She can do this.

The band strikes up "Till the End of Time." And I start to back away. Ben holds out his hand to Ruby Jane and leads her onto the dance floor. Fruit punch can wait.

Ruby Jane and her curls bounce to the center of the room.

My favorite dance partners bound over when the song ends, and Ben asks me to dance next.

"Me?"

"You."

"Oh. Okay."

He takes my right hand. It isn't hot in the cafeteria, but I feel warm.

Two steps into the dance, the band stops midsong.

Whispers fill the room and folks stand still. Randall Horton escorts Mama through the parting crowd.

Romeo? He's dressed as Romeo? With tights? A tunic? A sword?

He looks perfectly ridiculous.

"Now I've seen everything," says Ben.

Someone claps. Another joins in. Suddenly the whole room, except me, cheers.

This is not the plan.

Randall Horton bows to Mama. The band starts up. And they dance.

I flee to the bathroom.

The door swings open. Miss Connie and Ruby Jane's mama enter.

I slip into a stall before they can see me.

"*C'est l'amour,*" says Miss Connie. "Now, that is love. Randall Horton is a certified romantic."

"So creative," says Mrs. Pfluger. "I couldn't imagine why he needed Homer's plastic sword. Of course I said he could borrow it, especially since Randall harbored Homer and Ruby Jane in the pharmacy during the hailstorm last week."

That man ruins everything.

"May I have your attention, please," says Mr. McGrath from the bandstand, and he waits for a hush to come over the room.

"It is time to announce this year's Valentine royal couple."

Mr. James from the *Gladiola Gazette* has his camera ready.

I spot Delilah between Harry and her daddy.

"Will Miss Shelley Darrow and Mr. Howard Leavitt please come to the stage."

Delilah bites on her lower lip. She looks like someone stole her favorite baton.

Harry and her daddy talk to her from each side, and whatever they say helps her smile.

"There you are," says Mama as I skirt around the tables that ring the dance floor. "Have you said hello to Randall yet tonight?"

I wiggle my fingers in his direction.

"As you can see," says Mama, "Randall's starting a new tradition."

"It might catch on," he says with a wink to me.

He didn't tell her?

"Really?" I ask.

"Why not?" says Mama, linking her elbow in mine. "Now come on—it's photo time."

"Thanks," I mouth to Randall Horton as we head to the corner of the room.

Without missing a step, he does a quick bow from his waist.

Mama and Randall Horton are scheduled to take pictures for the next hour. Grandpa has painted the backdrop—a big red heart. He and Grams were the first duo on duty.

"As the designated photographer for a few more minutes," Grandpa says as we walk up, "I insist on a picture of you three."

Mama, Randall Horton, and I pose. I don't want to smile. However, Randall Horton just did me a favor and Grams is by Grandpa making funny faces.

Back home, Grams, Grandpa, Mama, and I place valentines under each other's pillows and say good night.

In my room, I sit at my desk and open their cards. Grandpa's is funny, and Mama's and Grams's are mushy.

I have one more valentine to sign—the best one of all. I reach for my pen and write, *I love you, Daddy. Your Glory Bea.*

I stand the card on the top of my dresser beside his photo and blow him a kiss. Sparkles of glitter sprinkle around him. A few stick to his picture. One settles over his heart.

"See you the day after tomorrow."

forty

TODAY IS the day.

A kaleidoscope-of-monarchs-in-my-stomach kind of day.

I ensure that my WELCOME HOME DADDY! poster is still under my bed. I'll retrieve it later and tape it to the railing upstairs.

I look out my bedroom window toward the train station and squint real good. I can make out the American flag waving on top of the building against the clear sky, all the way at the end of Main. Mr. McGrath was wrong about the weather.

"Blue-sky day, Daddy," I say, turning from the window to his picture. "Our favorite kind."

"Ready, sugar?" calls Mama.

My hair ribbon has vanished, but it is time to go.

I blow a kiss, grab my sack of confetti, and walk out of my room backward, my eyes still on him.

All of Gladiola will greet him. School's canceled and most businesses are closed.

"You look darling," Mama says after I fly down the banister. She gives me a hug and hands me my red ribbon. "I found it in the kitchen."

"Thanks," I say. "You look great too."

Like Mama, I am all decked out in red, white, and blue. Grams made us matching navy-blue dresses with white piping around the collar and cuffs. Red kerchiefs are tucked into our front pockets. Too bad we'll have to cover up our outfits with winter coats.

"Let's go," she says, handing me a small flag.

The parade will start in an hour, and Mama and I need to be early. We are riding in the car after the mayor and before the men from the American Legion. First I want to check out Ben and Grandpa's mystery float. And of course see if by any chance Daddy's come early.

Even though the sun is out, it's chilly. Now gray clouds sit on the horizon. I double-triple wrap my scarf around my neck. I link my arm in Mama's and huddle close as we make our way.

"What do you have in the bag, sweetheart?" asks Mama.

"A surprise for the VIP."

"Your daddy loved surprises," she says, and kisses me on the top of my head.

I want to tell Mama about Daddy's return right now. I can—I will—keep our secret secret a little longer.

In the parking lot of the Gladiola Recreation Center, Grandpa hollers into a megaphone, "First up, honor guard. Next, Uncle Sam and Lady Liberty, then . . ."

It looks like a big old mess to me—kids with dogs in wagons all decorated in flags, men and women in military uniforms, four different marching bands, floats of all shapes and sizes, riders on horseback, not to mention the Gerbera Daisies and Dudes and the Gladiola Glee Club—and Grandpa always keeps his cool. I know he will get everyone lined up.

I don't spot Grams or any other glee club members. Chances are they're still in the Rec Center warming up their voices.

But I do see Delilah in a sparkly outfit and white boots surrounded by little girls. One hands her an autograph book to sign. Mama says Delilah has more followers than friends. I think that must be true.

Ben said he'd station their float under a pecan tree at the far end of the lot. I look into the face of every man wearing a US Army uniform as I make my way. It would be just like Daddy to pop out of the crowd and say, "Surprise!" I'd love to surprise him first.

I'll recognize him, right? Maybe his hair is longer. Maybe I've grown so much, he'll hardly recognize me. Maybe he's hiding so he can make a big grand entrance in front of everyone.

I don't see my daddy. Instead, I see Ben.

He and others gather around a flatbed truck. A tall, silvery papier-mâché replica of the Eiffel Tower and two big French poodles wearing tilted black berets stand on top of a platform.

So that's what all the newspaper in the studio was for. Cardboard boxes covered with white butcher paper edge the truck bed. The writing on the boxes, painted blue, white, and red, just like the French flag, says, VIVE LA FRANCE.

"What do you say?" asks Ben as I walk up.

"Magnifique!"

Ben must be hot, because his face turns red.

"Open this later," he says, and hands me an envelope.

"Okay." I tuck it into my coat pocket.

Ben pulls a long, skinny blue balloon out of his pocket and blows it up. It looks like a gigantic frankfurter. In a blur, he twists it this way and that. He's a movie reel on fast-forward.

"Voilà," he says, and hands me a French poodle.

"Thank you. I mean, *merci*." I keep my head up, still looking for the most important face.

"Hi," says Ruby Jane, bouncing up. She grabs an inflated balloon from a box on the truck. "Guh-lore-ee-us day, isn't it?" she says, waving it like a conductor's baton.

"Best ever," I say.

I wander with my bag of confetti through the maze of folks milling in front of the Rec Center and circle back to the beginning of the parade, at the corner of State Street and Pecan Avenue. Uncle Sam and Lady Liberty chat with the flag bearers.

I weave down the lineup on Pecan Avenue. Past the Gladiola

High School marching band, decked out in their red-and-white uniforms with gold tassels on their shoulders. Past the twirlers in gold sequined costumes, dancing around with little white puffs of air streaming out of their mouths. Past the six women in military uniform, who are having their pictures taken by Mr. James from the *Gladiola Gazette*. Just beyond is a group of men in military uniforms, some of whom have joined us from out of town.

I can't get close enough. "HELLO," I holler. "I'm Glory Bea Bennett. Thank you for your service."

"You're welcome," a voice answers. It doesn't belong to the one I know.

Grandpa's five-minute warning whistle blows. I run to find Mama.

I never did see Grams.

Mama and I settle in on the top of the back seat of a new red convertible with red seats, from Crowley Motors. I leave plenty of room between us. My paper bag is on the floorboard.

I wave my flag in one hand and practice waving at the same time with the other.

"Remember to smile," Mama says, and inches closer.

The monarchs in my stomach are doing loop-the-loops. I stand to get an even better look around.

The sidewalks are empty. A few folks will be on State. Most will wait on Main.

In front of us Mr. and Mrs. Crowley climb into a new blue

convertible. Before them is Ben and Grandpa's float and the Drum Rollers, four high school boys with four humongous bass drums. In back of us, three men older than Grandpa hold a maroon-and-gold-colored banner from the American Legion waist high. It almost stretches across the whole street. Behind them, men from the First World War line up. One man has a sleeve of his uniform pinned up to his shoulder. Another holds a crutch under one arm.

Grandpa blows his whistle nine times, one for each hour. Mama tugs me to sit back down. The Gladiola High School band plays "America the Beautiful," and everyone starts to sing.

When our car finally turns on to Main Street, all I see is red, white, and blue bunting draped across the tops of all the buildings, and sidewalks with people four and five deep, waving flags and cheering. Some throw confetti and streamers.

For France. For Mama and me.

For my daddy.

At the train station way down at the end of the street, I see the train. On the track to the left of the main building, a small gray boxcar sits atop a flatbed. It's here! Now Daddy must be too!

I wave my flag as hard as I can. I spot Miss Connie and a man with a potbellied pig on a leash standing outside the pharmacy. It's Mr. Huckleberry from the Tula train station! Grams's fortieth miracle? From their faces, I'd say yes. Miss Connie points to the lady and a boy and a girl on the other side of her. The Huffmans!

"Mama, look," I say. "My friends from Tula."

Meredith holds up a balloon poodle and grins.

Ruby Jane stands in front of the Gladiola Theater with a bunch of kids from school. The marquee reads: BIENVENUE. WELCOME. She gives me a thumbs-up.

As we pass by the *Gladiola Gazette*, Mr. Wyatt and Mrs. Pfluger stand out front and signal their hellos.

Grams's glee club is a few groups ahead. She helped all the women with long hair fix it into chignons, which is French for "hair buns." The parade stops so the glee club can sing "My Country, 'Tis of Thee." Mama sings along.

I stand on the seat so I can see Daddy and he can see me. He's got to be here somewhere. There's only a couple of blocks to go.

On the other side of the street, a man in uniform leans beside the barber pole in front of Sam's Barber Shop holding a little girl in his arms. The woman next to him puts her arm around his waist. The man has red hair and a patch over one eye. He is not my daddy.

There's Ben's dad! He's in front of the Five & Dime variety store. In uniform. Standing with Ben's mom.

Ben tosses his half-made balloon poodle onto the float, grabs a small flag, and rushes to his dad. He hands the flag to him and salutes.

I must not be the only one who notices, because all around me, everyone turns to clap or salute too.

forty-one

THE PARADE ends at the train depot, where the gray Merci box-car, with its painted sash of blue, white, and red emblazoned with the words GRATITUDE TRAIN across it, sits atop a flatbed car just beyond the station. Fancy hand-painted wooden plaques deco-rate its sides. There is one plaque for each of France's provinces (which are like our states), plus a few extras for good measure.

With my paper bag in one hand, I push through the crowd. I reach up to touch a plaque with a gold-and-red-striped shield, but a line of men from town encircles the boxcar and they ask everyone to move away.

I hurry back to the station, climb onto a boulder next to the steps, and face the mass of people. Folks fill up every piece of ground and spill over onto Main Street. I shade my forehead with my hand and scan as many faces as I can.

"Glory Bea," Mama shouts. A group of hands reaches up a few feet away from me. Mama, Randall Horton, and Grams motion for me to join them.

"Not yet," I call. *Not till I find Daddy.*

The high school band strikes up "The Liberty Bell" march as Mr. Crowley passes out certificates to his committee members. Each one, including Grandpa, says a bunch of kind words and then sits on a folding chair on top of the platform. The rolled top of my paper bag is squishy and damp in my hand.

I don't know why it's taking so long. *Come on, Daddy. It's time.* I switch my bag from left to right.

Mr. Crowley makes a long speech and the Gladiola Glee Club sings "La Marseillaise."

"And now for our special guest," says Mr. Crowley.

Here he comes!

"It is my great pleasure to welcome Governor Jester!"

My paper bag falls to the ground. I don't mean to, but I forget to clap as the governor makes his way to the podium.

Daddy, where are you? You promised you'd come home. You've got to come home.

The preacher from Gladiola Methodist says a blessing in English and French. I don't bow my head or close my eyes. I keep looking for Daddy. He must be like the cherry on top of a float—saving the best for last.

Suddenly it's over. The boxcar is due in Austin shortly, so we must say au revoir.

The whistle blows.

I wave the best Bennett good-bye I can. *Where is he?*

Then I locate Mama. The sky is now cloudy and gray, and instead of warming up, it's getting colder.

"What's the rush, Glory Bea?" she asks as I hurry her along. "There'll be plenty of food for everyone at the Bar-B-Que."

I'm not hurrying because I'm hungry. It's because it's suddenly clear: if Daddy wasn't at the parade or in the boxcar, it's because he's waiting for us inside the school. Maybe he can't walk so good, so he had to stay inside. Maybe he just wanted to make the surprise extra special.

Smokey-sweet smells greet us. Brisket, sausage, chicken, potato salad, coleslaw, and a whole slew of tasty desserts line the long tables in the cafeteria. All the town cooks have made their signature recipes. Folks lean over the dishes and murmur their praises. I set my paper bag on the stage before we make our plates.

"Have you found your VIP yet?" Mama asks.

"So far he's a no-show."

"Don't give up hope."

"Thanks, Mama." I'll never give up.

After fixing our plates, Mama, Grams, Grandpa, and I walk to the gym and join the table with the McGraths and Randall Horton. The bag of confetti sits under me.

Grandpa digs into his slice of apple-cinnamon crumb pie. "If this isn't Sadie Jean's recipe, then my name isn't William Conrad Bennett."

I scan all the nearby tables. One table over sits Miss Connie and her new gentleman friend, Mr. Huckleberry, with his pet pig, and the Huffmans from Tula.

"Hello again," I say, and wave the Bennett wave. I keep looking around the room for that one unforgettable face.

Mrs. Huffman comes over. "We so enjoyed meeting your daughter last week," she tells Mama. "We'll have to get together once Lloyd returns. Glory Bea is interested in his amnesia."

"We all are," says Mama. "We're so happy that he found his way back home."

I'm looking everywhere except at Mrs. Huffman. There are so many people in here. But not the one I want to see the most.

"Glory Bea, you are acting like a jack-in-the-box," says Mama, putting her hand gently on my arm. "Sit still and eat."

"I'll be right back. There's someone I've got to find."

Mama shakes her head.

I clutch my paper bag, hug it close, and racewalk back to the cafeteria. A few pieces of confetti land on my shoes. It's okay. There's plenty left. Folks are still fixing their plates or coming back for seconds. Out the windows, raindrops fall.

"Glory Bea," hollers Homer, waving his railroad cap. "What did the big train call the little train?"

"Later," I reply, and keep going.

"No," hollers Homer. "Toot. He called him Toot."

I zip up and down the rows of food tables, trailing confetti.

The men have all taken off their hats, which makes it easier. Not everyone has a high forehead.

Where is he?

I rush back to the gym and walk from row to row.

I turn and stare at the wall. The writing above the basketball hoop reads HOME OF THE GLADIOLA GIANTS. I let the words go blurry and sharp, blurry and sharp.

"Any luck?" says Randall, coming up beside me. He carries a piece of apple-cinnamon crumb pie in each hand.

"I've got to go home," I say, and race to the double doors.

Just before I reach the opening, Ruby Jane stops me.

"Glory Bea!" she says, holding my arm. "I couldn't sleep last night, I was so excited."

"Me too," I say, shifting my weight from side to side. More confetti falls.

Ruby Jane fans her face with both hands. "I've been thinking about someone all day."

"Ruby Jane, listen, I've got to go. My daddy's not here yet, and I just figured out that he's waiting for me at home."

Ruby Jane's eyes widen and she gets real still.

"Oh, Glory Bea," she says, soft and wispy. "You don't really . . . ?"

It doesn't matter whether she believes or not.

I believe.

I turn and run. Run as fast as I can.

forty-two

HE IS NOT waiting for me on the front porch.

I drop my paper bag and fling open the door.

"Daddy. Daddy!" I call.

No answer.

I search everywhere. Downstairs. The musty attic, where Mama has stored his clothes. The bedrooms.

"Daddy!" I call again and again.

The kitchen, where his pecan pie awaits.

Grandpa's studio.

Finally, I retrieve my bag of confetti. Only, when I pick it up, the bottom falls out. Clumps of wet newspaper splat onto the porch, followed by a flutter of dry confetti.

I sit down on the bottom porch step, plunk my elbows onto my knees, and hang my head between my fists. Drops of left-over rain plop from the eaves onto my shoulders.

When are you coming, Daddy? I thought today was the day. I've been waiting so long. I just knew you were coming. Where are you? You belong here. With Mama and me.

I can't live without you.

I don't want to live without you.

I need you to come back.

Footsteps sound on the walk, and my heart tap-dances.

A man. Not in dress shoes. Not in tennis shoes. A man wearing boots. I close my eyes and I hold my breath as the shoes come closer and closer. They stop in front of me.

I open my eyes. Brown boots so shiny, I can see myself in them. The man is in uniform. A US Army Ranger uniform.

I look up.

"Glory Bea," says Randall Horton. "You must be cold." He takes off his jacket, with its striped bars on the chest and white armband with the red cross, and rests it over my shoulders.

I look straight into his eyes. "People get amnesia, you know. Look at what happened to Mr. Huffman. One day he didn't know his own name, where he lived, what job he had, or if he had a family. Then one day he did. He was reunited with his wife and children and is living happily ever after. Soldiers get captured. They get lost."

I am talking fast. So fast.

"Maybe my daddy's records got mixed up with someone else's. Maybe he lost his dog tags or had on the wrong ones. Maybe he was injured real bad, so bad that they had to do surgery on his face, which changed his looks, and because he didn't remember who he was, he didn't recognize himself—"

An ocean of tears flows down my cheeks and lands on Randall Horton's jacket.

"Glory Bea. I am so sorry." Randall Horton sits beside me and takes my hands in his. "I'd like to tell you a story. A true story about your daddy."

I nod.

"He was the bravest man I've ever known. He saved my life the day we landed on Omaha Beach. When we hit the shore, I tripped and swallowed half the English Channel. Your daddy picked me up and dragged me to safety. I wish I could have done the same for him."

"You should have."

"You're right. I was a medic. The truth is, I couldn't control what happened. Your daddy went back to help someone else. Enemy fire hit him. He was gone in an instant. He did not suffer."

Gone. Gone as in not coming home. Ever?

That's not possible.

"No. You're wrong."

"I wish I were."

I can't live without my daddy. Mama may be able to. Grams and Grandpa may be able to. Not me.

I don't want to live without him.

"No. No. No. NO!"

Randall Horton squeezes my hands.

Now I get it.

The truth is, there is no hope. There never was.

Daddy's never coming back on any train. Never ever.

I shut my eyes. Tight.

I knew "lost" *could* mean "dead." I knew "missing" *could* mean "gone forever." But why would I believe that about Daddy?

I am a Bennett.

I have audacious expectations.

It was easier to hope that he was still alive than believe that he was dead.

I pop my eyes open and look into Randall Horton's. "Why didn't they find him and send him home?"

"I'm going to say this as carefully as I can, Glory Bea." Randall Horton bows his head, then looks at me straight on. "A lot of soldiers are in graves marked 'unknown,' or may never be found. Believe me, they have not been forgotten."

"Why my daddy? Why not . . ."

"I've wondered the same thing, Glory Bea."

"I thought if I hoped and prayed enough, he would come back. I miss him. I love him. It isn't enough." I'm still crying, tears and snot everywhere. Randall gives me his handkerchief.

"Love is enough, Glory Bea. Always. Your daddy is right here, in your heart. He knew how much you loved him. He loved you and your mama that much back."

"I wanted a miracle," I say.

Randall Horton closes his eyes. "So did I."

We sit real quiet for a spell.

"Glory Bea, your daddy was the one who got a miracle. You."

forty-three

BEFORE I GO to bed, like always, I take off my charm bracelet and set it next to Daddy's photo. I kept my New Year's resolution, most days. His homecoming would have been the best. No matter what I did—learn French, dissuade Randall Horton, suggest "Blue Skies" for the parade, paint a picture, journey to Fort Worth, polish his shoes, save his shirts, buy bait, make confetti, and more—no matter how much I wished and hoped and dreamed and prayed, Daddy isn't coming back.

Grams says people choose to hear what they want to hear. Maybe Mama and Grandpa and Grams told me straight out. Or tried to tell me. I think the last is true for sure. I heard only what I wanted to hear.

I fold my hands and close my eyes.

"I know you're in heaven, Daddy," I say. "Which means, I think, that you can hear me. Maybe even see me. I will miss you forever. If you could have, you would have stayed alive. If you could have, you would have come back. You wouldn't have left me. Thank you for being my daddy. I will never forget you. *Merci*, Daddy. *Je t'aime*. I love you."

I reach for the envelope from Ben that I plunked onto my desk and pull out a heart-shaped card. *2 Good 2 B 4-Gotten*. I turn it over. The note on the back reads, *I hope you like what I left under the dining room chair. From, Ben.*

I run downstairs. All the chairs are in place. I don't see anything underneath any of them.

I hold the back of my chair. I pull it from the table, tip it over, and look underneath. Nothing. I go around the table. Grandpa's, Grams's, company's.

Daddy's.

Carefully I tilt Daddy's chair over so the top of the back touches the floor.

Oh!

Gold stars, the kind teachers use for their students' best work, circle the rim, framing my words—*Daddy was here*.

It looks like a movie marquee.

"I dreamed about your daddy last night," says Grams as she places a tender bunch of red lettuce from our garden into my basket the next day. It's brisk, sunny.

I haven't dreamed about my daddy ever. Not when I slept, anyway. I hardly ever remember my nighttime dreams.

I tighten my grip on my basket and sink to my knees.

"It's been a while," I say.

"At least a year or more."

"How did he look?" A quiet cool seeps from the ground into my legs.

Grams sits beside me and wraps her hands around mine on the basket handle.

"Your daddy looked so fine," she says. "He was wearing his blue-and-white aloha shirt."

"The one I helped you cut the other day," I say. I move my hands and grasp her hands. Grams and I talked Mama into making a quilt top out of some of Daddy's shirts. Someday soon, I'll be wrapping myself up in it with a book.

"The very one," Grams says, and moves my hands to her heart. "It was nighttime and we were all asleep. He opened my bedroom door and looked in at your grandpa and me. Then he went to your mama's room and yours and did the very same thing."

"He came home," I whisper, and let go of her hands.

"Yes, but not to stay."

"What do you mean?"

Grams lifts my chin and looks into my eyes. "There was one

more part, Glory Bea," she says, her voice trembling. "The last thing I saw, your daddy was walking in the clouds toward the gates of heaven."

I close my eyes and picture it, open them, and look at Grams. Her eyes glisten.

"The sign above the gates," she says softly, "read 'Home.'"

forty-four

"HAPPY BIRTHDAY!" Mama and Grams shout as Grandpa twirls me around the toasty-warm kitchen the next morning.

I hold on. Hold on tight.

"Is there such a thing as second chances?" I ask.

"Every day," he says. "No. Make that every second."

Birthdays at our house are a family celebration with a few invited guests. The honoree gets to pick out the dinner menu and request their favorite dessert. Everything else is a secret.

I have to stay in my room until the mystery guests arrive. The doorbell rings three times, and while I hear Grandpa say hello, the other person never says a word.

"President Truman, what an honor," Grandpa says.

Of course it isn't the president. It might be Ben or Randall Horton.

"Right this way, sir," says Grandpa. There are more than two sets of footsteps.

"Bob Mathias, congratulations on your gold medal last summer."

These folks are ones Grandpa would love at his party. I know who he'll say hello to next. Either Jack Benny, his favorite radio host, or the Andrews Sisters, his favorite singing group.

"LaVerne, Maxene, Patty, thank you for taking time from your tour to stop by. Glory Bea can't wait to see you."

No telling how many guests are really downstairs. For one of Grams's birthdays Grandpa opened the front door more than ten times. He kept me ringing the doorbell and walking in the front door and out the back. Finally, on the last ring, Grams's sister, all the way from California, entered. Grams said it was the best birthday she'd ever had.

"Glory Bea." Grandpa knocks on my bedroom door. "Your party awaits."

Arm in arm, Grandpa and I walk down the stairs. On the next-to-last step, we stop. Grandpa takes out his red bandana and wraps it over my eyes. It won't come off until we reach the dining room.

"Happy birthday!" everyone shouts.

I pull off my blindfold and look at Ruby Jane, Ben, Delilah, Randall Horton, and my family.

Ruby Jane and Ben! My first match. Together for one dance. And then not.

It turns out Ruby Jane likes Toby the valentine sender better. His favorite board game is Parcheesi. "You're a crummy matchmaker," she tells me. "Open your eyes."

Maybe matchmaking doesn't run in my family after all.

"Thanks for coming, everyone," I say.

Grandpa pulls out my chair and I sit.

"Ben," I say, pointing to the chair next to me.

He smiles real big and takes the seat.

"As is our tradition," says Grandpa, "we will begin with dessert."

On cue, Grams swoops in with a tray of Dr Pepper floats and sets it before me.

Mama lights the twelve candles on the confections. I wish a special wish and blow them all out.

Our table is full up. I look at the chair between Grams and Ben, Daddy's chair, and catch Randall Horton's eyes. He gives me two thumbs-up.

"How did you know?" I ask Ben as we eat, nodding toward my daddy's chair.

"X-ray vision."

"Ben." I bump my shoulder against his. "No, really. How?"

Ben looks right at me. The flecks of gold in his brown eyes match his shirt. "I saw the writing when I picked up the ice cube you put down my back."

"Ahhhh," I say. "Good eyes."

"Told you." He laughs and bumps his shoulder against mine.

After the floats, we dive into spaghetti and meatballs.

"Grams, this is the best meal ever," I say.

"I'm glad you've enjoyed it, Glory Bea. I'm not the one to thank."

"Mama?"

"Afraid not," she says. "Randall deserves all the credit."

I don't understand.

"Ben's dad has been giving me lessons," says Randall Horton. "I thought they might come in handy."

"Thank you from all of us," I say.

Everyone, including Mama, laughs.

"Shall we move to the parlor so the birthday girl can open her gifts?" asks Mama.

Ben picks up his plate and heads toward the kitchen.

"Arthur Benjamin Truman," says Grams. "You leave that be."

"Who?" I ask.

Ben puts down his plate.

"You?" I ask. "You are Arthur Benjamin?"

That is the name I saw on Grams's notepad by the phone. The one she takes notes on for her clients.

Ben shrugs. "My mama thought it sounded distinguished."

Since when does Grams give advice about crushes? Wait. Folks come to her, not vice versa. Which means Ben asked.

I open my cards and presents. I get lipstick from Ruby Jane, which makes Mama sigh and say something about not being able to wear lipstick before she was sixteen. Ben gives me a fancy pen.

"I notice you like to write things down," he says.

"I do," I say. "Thank you."

Ruby Jane places fingers on either side of her eyes and opens them extra wide. "Ben likes you," she mouths.

He does. And I'm just now seeing it. I turn to Grams and she winks.

Delilah gives me hair ribbons. Mama, Grams, and Grandpa give me a radio of my very own.

There is one more gift. Only, it has no tag or card. I tear into the wrapping and open the book.

"*The Secret Garden*," I say, and hug it to my chest.

"Do you like it?" asks Mama.

"Yes," I say. "Now I won't need to check it out again from the library. Thank you."

"I'm not the one to thank," she says.

I open the cover. The inscription in block letters reads: *Happy Birthday, Glory Bea! From, Randall.*

"Thank you . . . Randall."

Ruby Jane is the last to leave.

"I really did like him," she says as we stand in the parlor and ponder the Wall of Fame.

"I know. I'm sorry it didn't work out with Ben." I touch Ruby Jane's arm. "I promise, I didn't realize he liked me."

She rubs her forehead. "Glory Bea, you're fired. Again."

"Thank you," I say, and we burst into laughter. "I've decided to retire. You are—I mean, you were—my only client. In spite of my valentine cards advertising, no one else has requested my help."

My friend points to the NEVER GIVE UP pillow. "What about your motto?"

"Sometimes you need to change the plan."

Ruby Jane helps me tote my gifts upstairs.

I reach under my bed and pull out my painting for Daddy. "Would you help me hang this on my wall?" I hold it out to her.

"All that blue," says Ruby Jane.

"I made this for my daddy's homecoming. I'm one hundred and ten percent sure now, Ruby Jane."

"He would have loved it," she says.

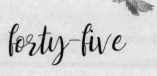

forty-five

February 21, 1949

Dear Texas Gratitude Train Committee,

My name is Glory Bea Bennett. My
daddy was Second Lieutenant George
Bennett from Gladiola, Texas. He served
in the US Army Rangers during WWII.
He died on Omaha Beach. I am writing to
request that my mama wear the wedding dress
from the Texas Merci boxcar on her wedding
day. I read about all the dresses from France
in the *Gladiola Gazette* earlier this year. Last
week I saw a picture of the Texas dress in the
newspaper. It will look beautiful on her.

Any day now Randall Horton, my daddy's best friend in the service, who hails from Brooklyn and is now a proud resident and pharmacist in Gladiola, will ask Mama to marry him. She will say yes.

My mama is the best mama in the whole world and she married the best man in the world, my daddy. Unfortunately, he left unexpectedly.

Now Mama has a second chance. So do I. I am very happy for her. For us.

Please consider Lila June Bennett for this gift. I have the support of your esteemed committee member Mrs. Geraldine Crowley, from my hometown.

I have enclosed a photo of Mama and me and Randall Horton. The original is on my dresser next to a picture of my daddy. This one was taken on Valentine's Day. Yes, Randall Horton dressed up as Romeo. Look at how happy Mama is. This is not a movie kind of love. It is true.

Sincerely yours,
Glory Bea Bennett

forty-six

I OPEN the front door, and the sun pours in. A whole month has passed since my birthday. It feels like spring.

"Mrs. Crowley," I say. "Please come in."

"Thank you. I'm here to see you and your mama."

"I'm right here," Mama says, setting on the front table a vase overflowing with sweet-smelling lilies that Randall just brought over.

Mrs. Crowley wears a lime-colored hat, white gloves, and a smile. She carries a big straw bag.

Is this Mama's lucky day?

"As you are aware, Lila June," says Mrs. Crowley, settling in on the sofa in the parlor, "I am on the governor's Texas Gratitude Train Committee."

Mama takes a seat in Daddy's leather chair, and I perch on

the needlepoint footstool beside it. A small breeze moves the sheer curtains beside me.

Hurry up, Mrs. Crowley. Tell her the good news. Tell her now.

"What you may not know, Lila June, is that your daughter wrote a letter to the train committee requesting that you wear the bride's dress from the boxcar."

"I had no idea," says Mama. She leans over me, wraps her arms around my shoulders, and rocks me side to side.

I reach for her arms.

Mrs. Crowley twists her wedding ring. "I am ever so sorry to tell you that the committee has declined the request."

"What?" I say. I throw off Mama's arms and stand. "That can't be. My mama should wear that dress. She deserves to wear that dress. Mrs. Crowley, please, make them change their minds."

The mayor's wife clears her throat. "As you may be aware, Lila June," she says, looking Mama in the eyes, "all the gifts are for display in a museum. Though, a few items may be auctioned. Not, of course, the wedding dress. I'd hoped we could make an exception to the rule, at least for one day. However, at the time of our decision, you were not engaged. No matter how persuasive Glory Bea's letter was, I was not able to sway the other members on your behalf."

"But—" I say.

"It was certainly an honor to be considered," says Mama,

and she clasps my hand. "Thank you for coming this afternoon to tell us this news in person."

"It is a shame," says Mrs. Crowley, "since I understand you and Randall Horton made it official yesterday. Please let Mr. Crowley and me be the first to say how happy we are for you. Let's set a date for that party."

"Thank you. I will pass your kind words on to Randall. He's out back fixing a window screen with Mr. Bennett and Ben Truman."

"However," says Mrs. Crowley, sitting up straighter, "the committee was so moved by Glory Bea's letter that we have decided to make an exception and give her one of the gifts instead."

"A gift for me? It should be Mama's."

"I must abide by the committee's wishes," says Mrs. Crowley. "Of course you may share it with whomever you wish."

I squeeze Mama's hand.

Mrs. Crowley continues, "Mr. James from the *Gladiola Gazette* is on your front porch and would like to take a picture of this momentous occasion."

"I'll let him in," says Mama, rising.

"Everyone," I call, as if they can hear me outside. "Come quick."

"Why don't you sit beside me, Glory Bea?" Mrs. Crowley pats the space next to her on the sofa.

A gift? From France?

It seems like it takes them forever. Finally Mama, Grams, Grandpa, Randall, Ben, and Mr. James gather around.

Mrs. Crowley reaches into her giant straw bag to pull out the gift. Mr. James says, "Say cheese, Glory Bea," and the camera flashes.

I blink away the stars and look at Mrs. Crowley's hands.

In them is a wooden box about the size of Grams's bread loaf pan. The tag attached to the top features three flowers the colors of the French flag blooming in front of a steam engine on a blue-sky day.

"On behalf of the Texas Gratitude Train Committee, it is my honor to present to you, Glory Bea Bennett, this thank-you gift from the people of France."

Mrs. Crowley places the box in my hands. It is heavy. I set it in my lap.

"Read the tag," says Grams.

"From Jean-Claude Pugeat," I say, "Bayeux, France."

"Imagine that, all the way from France," says Grandpa. "You going to open it?"

I unlatch the small clasp at the front and open the lid.

"Oh," I say. I reach my hand inside. "Sand." It is soft and warm. I swim my fingers through the fine grains of light brown.

"Well, I'll be," says Grams.

A thin blue envelope is tucked into the bottom of the lid.

"Hope it's in English," says Grams.

"Here's the letter opener," says Mama, holding up the one

with the green glass handle she keeps by Daddy's leather chair. "I'll be your translator if need be, sugar."

I smile my thanks.

Grandpa reaches for Grams's hand. Mr. James scribbles something in his spiral.

Mrs. Crowley fans her face. Ben hovers beside me.

I curl my hand tight around the smooth handle to stop the shaking and slide it through the longest side of the thin blue paper. I look up and Mama nods. Randall stands behind her with his hands on her shoulders.

I open the letter slowly so as not to make a tear.

"English," I say, and read aloud:

Dear American,

My name is Jean-Claude Pugeat. I am French. I am twelve years old. I am old enough to remember the war. I am very thankful your soldiers rescued my family, my country. I am thankful for the food we received from America.

Merci beaucoup, thank you very much.

I did not have money to buy something fancy. My papa made the wooden box. I used to fill it with toy soldiers. When the Nazis came to our farm, they threw the toys *onto the floor and smashed them with their hard boots.*

This gift of sand is from me. It is from a beach not far away.

In French the name of the beach is Vierville-sur-Mer. When the Americans came, they called it Omaha.

Your friend,
Jean-Claude

"Hooyah," whispers Ben.

I look up. Mama blows me a kiss. And outside the window behind her and Randall, a bird soars against the bright blue sky.

Sand. Sand from my daddy's beach. The very sand he walked on.

My daddy has come home.

author's note

Through a grassroots effort spearheaded by journalist and radio commentator Drew Pearson, Americans gathered and shipped freight cars full of food and goods to the people of Italy and France to help them recover from the devastation of World War II. They called it the Friendship Train. In response, French rail worker Andre Picard organized a campaign for the citizens of France to offer their thanks. Originally envisioned as one forty-and-eight boxcar filled with gifts of appreciation, the outpouring was so enormous that forty-nine boxcars were filled. They arrived in the United States in February 1949. Each state received a boxcar, and Washington, DC, and the Territory of Hawaii shared one. In each was a handmade wedding dress from seamstresses in Leon, a Sèvres vase from the French president, and thousands of individual gifts such as books, paintings, and toys.

Two hundred thousand people gathered for a ticker tape parade in New York City to welcome all the boxcars on February 3, 1949. Individual states then arranged for celebrations upon arrival of their boxcars. The Texas boxcar had a grand celebration in Fort Worth on February 14, 1949, and then headed south to Austin. It arrived in the capital city on Wednesday, February 16.

Some of the forty-nine boxcars still exist, along with a selection of their gifts. The Texas Merci boxcar, resplendent with its forty plaques representing provinces and cities in France, plus two more, is on permanent exhibit at the Texas Military Forces Museum at Camp Mabry in Austin. A sampling of gifts is a part of the Briscoe Center for American History at the University of Texas at Austin.

In addition, a book of thank-yous, signed by the people of France, is in the Personal Papers of Drew Pearson at the LBJ Library at the University of Texas at Austin, along with Pearson radio scripts, letters, telegrams, memos, newspaper articles, and more that detail the Merci Train effort. The Texas State Library and Archives Commission in Austin contains documentation of legislative efforts and correspondence to and from Governor Jester regarding the Texas boxcar. Lastly, the Personal Papers of Drew Pearson at the American University in Washington, DC, has archived Pearson's syndicated column and a selection of his radio broadcasts.

This novel is a work of fiction inspired by the Merci Train. In this story, the Texas boxcar makes a stop in the small town of

Gladiola before it arrives in Austin. Gladiola, Texas, the town of Tula, and all their residents exist only in my imagination.

Ben's dad, who served in World War II, suffered "shell shock." Today we would call it PTSD, post-traumatic stress disorder. Then, there was less support for veterans when they returned home.

The United States lost more than four hundred thousand service members in World War II. More than seventy-two thousand are still missing.

SELECTED BIBLIOGRAPHY

Adair, A. Garland. "French Box Car Is in Austin's Shrine." *Austin Statesman*, September 17, 1949.

Defense POW/MIA Accounting Agency. "World War II Accounting." United States Department of Defense. https://www.dpaa.mil/Our-Missing /World-War-II/.

Hadler, Susan Johnson, and Ann Bennett Mix, comps. *Lost in the Victory: Reflections of American War Orphans of World War II*. Edited by Calvin L. Christman. Denton, Texas: University of North Texas Press, 1998.

Hart, Weldon. Telegram, Weldon Hart to unknown. "French Thank You Train." Archives and Information Services Division, Texas State Library and Archives Commission.

Hendricks, Bill. Letter, Bill Hendricks to Drew Pearson, January 20, 1949. "French Train—Administrative," Personal Papers of Drew Pearson, Box F 125 (4 of 4), LBJ Library.

Jester, Beauford H. "Proclamation by the Governor of the State of Texas re the 'Train of Gratitude.'" Attached to a letter from G. Ward Moody of the American Legion Department of Texas, August 27, 1948. Archives and Information Services Division, Texas State Library and Archives Commission.

Livre d'or: Hommage de Paris et de l'Île-de-France au peuple Américain, Train de la Reconnaissance Française MCMXLIX. Personal Papers of Drew Pearson, Box G 312 (3 of 3), LBJ Library.

Merci Train (website). Updated 2019. www.mercitrain.org.

"'Merci' Train Will Roll in This Morning." *Austin Statesman*, February 16, 1949.

"Midwest Schedule of Merci Train," undated memo. "Railroad Schedules & Correspondence," Personal Papers of Drew Pearson, Box F 125 (4 of 4), LBJ Library.

Pearl Harbor Visitors Bureau. "Pearl Harbor Ships on the Morning of the Attack." Updated 2019. https://visitpearlharbor.org/pearl-harbor-ships -on-december-7th/.

Pearson, Drew. *The Washington Merry-Go-Round* (January 29, 1949). Drew Pearson's Washington Merry-Go-Round collection. American University Library Special Collections Unit, American University. https:// auislandora-stage.wrlc.org/islandora/object/pearson%3A11980#page /1/mode/1up.

———. Radio Script. ABC. January 9, 1949. "Radio Scripts: Jan-Feb-Mar 1949," Personal Papers of Drew Pearson. Box G 179 (1 of 3), LBJ Library.

Raaen, John C., Jr. "5th Battalion." Descendants of WWII Rangers, Inc. Updated 2018. http://www.wwiirangers.org/our-history/ranger-history /5th-btn/.

Rowe, Abbie, photographer. *Photograph of boxcar from French "Merci train," a gift from France to the United States in grateful recognition of U.S. aid to France after World War II, during a ceremony.* February 6, 1949. Photograph. Audiovisual Collection, 1957–2006. National Archives and Records Administration, Harry S. Truman Library, Independence, MO. http://catalog.archives.gov/id/200078.

Scheele, Dorothy R. The Friendship Train of 1947 (website). Updated 2017. http://www.thefriendshiptrain1947.org.

Seigel, Kalman. "City Roars Thanks to France for Car of Gratitude Train." *New York Times*, February 4, 1949.

Skouras, Spyros. Letter, Spyros Skouras to Drew Pearson, December 7, 1948. "French Train—Administrative," Personal Papers of Drew Pearson, Box F 125 (4 of 4), LBJ Library.

Texas (State). Legislature. House. Merci Train—Display of Gifts. 51st Legislature. H.C.R. No. 62 (1949). The Portal to Texas History. Digital Libraries Division, University of North Texas Libraries, Denton, TX. http://

texashistory.unt.edu/ark:/67531/metapth307687/m1/1479/zoom/?q=Merci%20Train%20and%20Gratitude%20Train%20and%201949&resolution=4.720367576335451&lat=3562.5&lon=750.

"Time Frames: Merci Train." *Fort Worth Star-Telegram*, November 25, 2015. http://www.star-telegram.com/news/local/community/article46580340.html.

"'What Happens If I Don't Have a Ticket?' Early State Law Was Alarmingly Specific." History Corner. *The Call Board: Newsletter of the Austin Steam Train Association*, Winter 2018, No. 88. Austin Steam Train Association, Cedar Park, TX. https://www.austinsteamtrain.org/cms/assets/uploads/2018/02/Call-Board-Winter-2018-88.pdf.

ACKNOWLEDGMENTS

Bouquets of thanks to everyone who has journeyed beside me as I wrote this book. It's taken over fifteen years to become this novel. I couldn't have done it without the support and love and brainpower of so many. I am forever grateful. It is the story of my heart.

Marsha Sharp, now retired educational specialist from the LBJ Library, facilitated my discovery of the Gratitude Train and the Texas boxcar. That led to my first drafts of a picture book read by the always fabulous Cynthia Leitich Smith and Kathi Appelt. The awesome Austin writing community encouraged me from the start. This book wouldn't exist without all of them. *Merci beaucoup.*

I treasure the rejection letter from former editor Amy Hsu, who suggested I reenvision my picture book submission as a novel. Only how was I going to do that? With a trainload of help from my VCFA (Vermont College of Fine Arts) advisors Ellen Howard, Sharon Darrow, Martine Leavitt, and Shelley Tanaka; fellow students; librarians in various archival collections; the mercitrain .org website; and more, I began again and reshaped the story into a middle-grade manuscript. Only a variation of the letter from Jean-Claude survived the transformation. Thank you, all.

As often happens in the life of a writer, that manuscript wasn't a match for those I queried, so I set it aside. More years passed. I kept writing and sold two books. Then I sunk to a creative low. I asked myself two questions: Did I still want to write? Yes. And, if I could only work on one more story, which would it be? I knew instantly.

With the help of my magnificent agent, Emily Wood Mitchell, and fantastic writers Kathi Appelt, Meredith Davis, Susan Fletcher, Lindsey Lane, and Liz Garton Scanlon, I revised Glory Bea's story again and again. Wonderful writers Varsha Bajaj, Cate Berry, Paige Britt, Donna Janell Bowman, and Carmen Oliver offered heartfelt support. *Merci, merci.*

I also researched more. Thanks ever so much to the exceedingly helpful librarians at the LBJ Library Reading Room, Briscoe Center for American History at the University of Texas at Austin, Texas State Archives Commission, and Austin History Center. And to Lil Serafine, executive director at the Austin Steam Train Association, who gave me a private tour of a restored car from the Texas Eagle train. If I made any missteps, they are on me.

Thank you, Grand Voiture du Texas, caretakers of the Texas Merci boxcar, now situated at the Texas Military Forces Museum at Camp Mabry. I love to visit.

In addition, BJ, Charles, and Annie Holcomb, I am grateful for your enthusiasm for this story. Kathleen Davis Niendorff, for your insights and belief that it would find a home. The St. Matthew's Bible study, for your prayers. Joan and Jerry Andersen, for being a phone call away. Karen and Eric Braunsdorf, for boundless interest and gifts, and Ray and Cristy Pfeiffer, for your historic tour of Normandy.

Agent Emily Wood Mitchell found the most perfect editor, Krista Vitola, who, along with other dream makers at Simon & Schuster Books for Young Readers, such as publisher Justin Chanda, associate editor Catherine Laudone, book designer Lizzy Bromley, jacket artist Dung Ho Hanh, copy editors Stephanie Evans, Dorothy Gribbin, and Alison Velea, and proofreader Bara MacNeill, gave their all. Likewise, the top-notch school and library marketing team of Michelle Leo, Sarah Woodruff, and Amy Beaudoin and my publicist Audrey French have been and still are hard at work. This entire process has been divine. I can't thank you all enough.

My parents are gone, but I am indebted to them as well. Before they married, they both served in World War II. Afterward, I was born and raised (mostly) in Hawaii. I grew up on tours of Pearl Harbor and stories of December 7, 1941. Because of this, I've always felt connected to the war and its effects. My dad and I had a very special connection and I've missed him every day since he passed. He loved blue-sky days.

My final thank-yous are to my husband, Lane, and his incredible family, who welcomed me in and cheer me on. I love y'all.

A READING GROUP GUIDE TO

Blue Skies

by Anne Bustard

About the Book

The war ended three years ago, but Glory Bea's father never returned home from France. Glory Bea understands what Mama, Grams, and Grandpa say—that Daddy died a hero on Omaha Beach—yet, deep down in her heart, she believes that Daddy is still out there. When she hears that one of the boxcars from the Merci (or "thank you") Train—a train filled with gifts of gratitude from the people of France—will be stopping in her town of Gladiola, Texas, she just knows that her daddy will be its surprise cargo.

Discussion Questions

1. *Blue Skies* is historical fiction. Have you read any other novels in this genre? How do you feel about stories that are based on real events? Does that change your reading

experience, or how you view the characters? Please explain your answers.

2. Describe the book's time period. How can you tell that it's set during a specific time? Please explain your answer using examples from the text. How does it affect the novel's events? Have you read other historical fiction or nonfiction books about WWII? What elements would you like to know more about?

3. If you were to write a historical fiction story, what time period would you set it in? What periods in history are the most interesting to you? Please explain your answer. What books or articles have you read about these time periods? Where would you go to find more information?

4. Who is your favorite character in the book? Who most reminds you of someone in your own life? Discuss some of the character descriptions. Do you think people have similar character traits across time periods?

5. If you lived in Glory Bea's town during this time, what would you miss most about your current life? What would you be most excited to experience?

6. Talk about how Ben's loss differs from Glory Bea's. Which do you think would be harder—to never see your father again, or to have him return as a different man? Why do you think war might cause someone to change? What do you think might have happened to Mr. Truman?

7. Gladiola, Texas, has a population of 3,421. Do you know

the population of your town? How far are you from the nearest city? Talk about some of the ways that big cities and small towns are different. Do you prefer one over the other? Please explain your answers. Do you think the plot of *Blue Skies* would have changed if Glory Bea had lived in a larger town?

8. On New Year's Eve, Glory Bea's family spends the evening at home, waiting for midnight. What do they do for entertainment? What does this tell you about their relationships or their lifestyle? How does this differ from how some families celebrate today? Does your family have a New Year's Eve tradition?

9. For most of the book, Glory Bea is certain that her father will return home. It was not unusual for WWII orphans to sustain this fantasy. How did you feel about her beliefs? Were you hopeful, or were you afraid she would be disappointed? If you were Glory Bea's friend, what would you have said to her? Please explain your answers.

10. Ruby Jane refers to Glory Bea's father, asking, "'What if he's gone for good?'" Do you think Ruby Jane is right to be honest? Do you think Ruby Jane is trying to be a good friend? How does Glory Bea react? What would you have done if you were in Ruby Jane's shoes?

11. Grams says that her matchmaking is "a calling." What does she mean by that? Do you agree with her analysis? Please explain your answer. What do you think are the

differences between a calling and a hobby? Give examples from your own experiences, or from those of family and friends.

12. Did you suspect the reason for Glory Bea's rocky attempt at matchmaking? Would you ever try to play matchmaker for one of your friends? How might that turn out? Have you learned any tips or pitfalls from Glory Bea's experiences?

13. Discuss how the author introduces us to Daddy without ever allowing us to meet him. What do we learn about him from Glory Bea, Grams, and Randall Horton? Do you feel like you have a full picture of what he was like? Please explain your answer.

14. Why does Glory Bea dislike Randall Horton? Do you agree with Grams when she says, "'No matter how much you don't like someone, you can always discover one thing about them to appreciate'"? What might you tell Glory Bea to appreciate about Randall Horton? What might he appreciate about Glory Bea?

15. How does patriotism play a part in this story? Give examples from the text. What does patriotism mean to Glory Bea? What does it mean to you? Compare patriotism in Gladiola with contemporary America. How does each place demonstrate patriotism?

16. Can you name some of the French words used in the book? How did you use context to determine their mean-

ings? Had you heard any of them before? What other French words or phrases do you know, or would like to learn?

17. Glory Bea is thrilled when she thinks she spots her daddy in the newsreel about the Merci Train. Do you know what a newsreel is? Discuss how different it would be to get most of your news from the radio or newsreels. How do you and your family get news of world events?

18. At the beginning of the book, readers learn one of Grams's expressions: "Have audacious expectations." What does audacious mean? How might you have audacious expectations? Talk about the benefits and dangers of expecting things will turn out for the best. If Glory Bea hadn't been expecting her daddy to arrive on the Merci Train, do you think she could have avoided disappointment? Or was it important for her to have that hope?

Extension Activities

1. Write an essay about how the author exhibits the theme of "blue skies" throughout the book. Give examples from the text to support your conclusions.

2. The book's bibliography includes many articles and books about the real Merci Train. Choose a state other than Texas; then research and write a report about the Merci Train's visit and the gifts distributed there. How are other experiences similar to or different from Glory Bea's?

3. Reread chapters forty and forty-one and then write an essay about how the author uses the parade setting to reflect some of the book's themes.

4. Pretend you are a reporter for the *Gladiola Gazette* and write an article about the Merci Train's visit. Which facts would you include? Who in the town would you interview? What kind of emotions are you hoping to evoke?

5. Research and write a report about the WWII battle at Omaha Beach, where Glory Bea's father died. What information are you most surprised about? Which information was hardest to read?

6. Make a poster advertising the arrival of the Merci Train in Gladiola. Bonus for using the French flag, the Texas flag, and some French words! Hang the posters in your classroom, and discuss the various interpretations.

7. Pretend you are Glory Bea and write an entry in your diary about Randall Horton on the day that he uses the special family wave.

Guide written by Bobbie Combs, a consultant at We Love Children's Books.

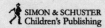

★ "A must for readers who
appreciate a heartfelt mystery."
—*Booklist* (starred review)

Just
South
of
Home

KAREN STRONG

"Every bit as magical as the Miracles the town is famous for. Stacy Hackney explores faith, family, and community with humor and heart in this lovely debut."

—CINDY BALDWIN, author of *Where the Watermelons Grow*

PRINT AND EBOOK EDITIONS AVAILABLE
From Simon & Schuster Books for Young Readers
simonandschuster.com/kids

A novel about sisterhood, friendship,
and the small moments that mean
everything, from the author of
If This Were a Story.

THE
LAST
TREE TOWN

Beth Turley
Author of *If This Were a Story*

PRINT AND EBOOK EDITIONS AVAILABLE
From Simon & Schuster Books for Young Readers
simonandschuster.com/kids

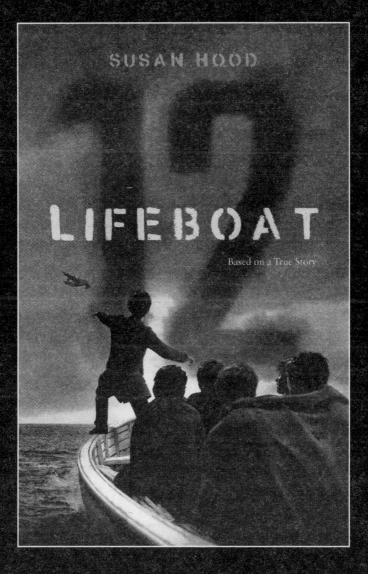

"This page-turning true-life adventure is filled with rich and riveting details and a timeless understanding of the things that matter most."
—Dashka Slater, author of *The 57 Bus*

SUSAN HOOD

LIFEBOAT

Based on a True Story